PENGUIN CRIME FICTION

Editor: Julian Symons

THE SCANDAL
OF FATHER BROWN

G. K. Chesterton was born in 1874, and educated at St Paul's School, where, despite his efforts to achieve honourable oblivion at the bottom of his class, he was singled out as a boy with distinct literary promise. He decided to follow art as a career, and studied at the Slade School, where, while 'attending or not attending to his studies', he met Ernest Hodder-Williams, who formed the fixed notion that Chesterton could write. At his request he reviewed a number of books for the *Bookman* and found himself launched on a profession he was to follow all his life. Probably his most famous stories are those of 'Father Brown', but he wrote much about every conceivable subject under or beyond the sun. The best accounts of his life are to be found in his own *Autobiography*, published soon after his death in 1936, and in Miss Maisie Ward's *Life* of him. Many of his books have been issued as Penguins.

THE SCANDAL
OF FATHER BROWN

G. K. CHESTERTON

PENGUIN BOOKS

Penguin Books Ltd, Harmondsworth, Middlesex, England
Penguin Books, 625 Madison Avenue, New York, New York 10022, U.S.A.
Penguin Books Australia Ltd, Ringwood, Victoria, Australia
Penguin Books Canada Ltd, 2801 John Street, Markham, Ontario, Canada L3R 1B4
Penguin Books (N.Z.) Ltd, 182–190 Wairau Road, Auckland 10, New Zealand

—

First published by Cassell 1929
Published in Penguin Books 1978
Copyright the Estate of G. K. Chesterton
All rights reserved

—

Made and printed in Great Britain by
C. Nicholls & Company Ltd
The Philips Park Press, Manchester
Set in Monotype Times

Contents

ONE

The Scandal of Father Brown

It would not be fair to record the adventures of Father Brown, without admitting that he was once involved in a grave scandal. There still are persons, perhaps even of his own community, who would say that there was a sort of blot upon his name. It happened in a picturesque Mexican road-house of rather loose repute, as appeared later; and to some it seemed that for once the priest had allowed a romantic streak in him, and his sympathy for human weakness, to lead him into loose and unorthodox action. The story in itself was a simple one; and perhaps the whole surprise of it consisted in its simplicity.

Burning Troy began with Helen; this disgraceful story began with the beauty of Hypatia Potter. Americans have a great power, which Europeans do not always appreciate, of creating institutions from below; that is by popular initiative. Like every other good thing, it has its lighter aspects; one of which, as has been remarked by Mr Wells and others, is that a person may become a public institution without becoming an official institution. A girl of great beauty or brilliancy will be a sort of uncrowned queen, even if she is not a Film Star or the original of a Gibson Girl. Among those who had the fortune, or misfortune, to exist beautifully in public in this manner, was a certain Hypatia Hard, who had passed through the preliminary stage of receiving florid compliments in society paragraphs of the local press, to the position of one who is actually interviewed by real pressmen. On War and Peace and Patriotism and Prohibition and Evolution and the Bible she had made her pronouncements with a charming smile; and if none of them seemed very near to the real grounds of her own reputation, it was almost equally hard to say what the grounds of her reputation really were. Beauty, and being the daughter of a rich man, are things not rare

7

in her country; but to these she added whatever it is that attracts the wandering eye of journalism. Next to none of her admirers had even seen her, or even hoped to do so; and none of them could possibly derive any sordid benefit from her father's wealth. It was simply a sort of popular romance, the modern substitute for mythology; and it laid the first foundations of the more turgid and tempestuous sort of romance in which she was to figure later on; and in which many held that the reputation of Father Brown, as well as of others, had been blown to rags.

It was accepted, sometimes romantically, sometimes resignedly, by those whom American satire has named the Sob Sisters, that she had already married a very worthy and respectable business man of the name of Potter. It was even possible to regard her for a moment as Mrs Potter, on the universal understanding that her husband was only the husband of Mrs Potter.

Then came the Great Scandal, by which her friends and enemies were horrified beyond their wildest hopes. Her name was coupled (as the queer phrase goes) with a literary man living in Mexico; in status an American, but in spirit a very Spanish American. Unfortunately his vices resembled her virtues, in being good copy. He was no less a person than the famous or infamous Rudel Romanes; the poet whose works had been so universally popularized by being vetoed by libraries or prosecuted by the police. Anyhow, her pure and placid star was seen in conjunction with this comet. He was of the sort to be compared to a comet, being hairy and hot; the first in his portraits, the second in his poetry. He was also destructive; the comet's tail was a trail of divorces, which some called his success as a lover and some his prolonged failure as a husband. It was hard on Hypatia; there are disadvantages in conducting the perfect private life in public; like a domestic interior in a shop-window. Interviewers reported doubtful utterances about Love's Larger Law of Supreme Self-Realization. The Pagans applauded. The Sob Sisterhood permitted themselves a note of romantic regret; some having even the hardened audacity to quote from the poem of Maud Mueller, to the effect that of all the words of tongue or pen, the saddest are 'It might have been.' And Mr Agar P. Rock, who hated the Sob Sisterhood with a holy and righteous hatred, said that in this case he thoroughly agreed with Bret Harte's emendation of the poem: 'More sad are those we daily see; it is, but it hadn't ought to be.'

For Mr Rock was very firmly and rightly convinced that a very large number of things hadn't ought to be. He was a slashing and savage critic of national degeneration, on the *Minneapolis Meteor*, and a bold and honest man. He had perhaps come to specialize too much in the spirit of indignation, but it had had a healthy enough origin in his reaction against sloppy attempts to confuse right and wrong in modern journalism and gossip. He expressed it first in the form of a protest against an unholy halo of romance being thrown round the gunman and the gangster. Perhaps he was rather too much inclined to assume, in robust impatience, that all gangsters were Dagos and that all Dagos were gangsters. But his prejudices, even when they were a little provincial, were rather refreshing after a certain sort of maudlin and unmanly hero-worship, which was ready to regard a professional murderer as a leader of fashion, so long as the pressmen reported that his smile was irresistible or his tuxedo was all right. Anyhow, the prejudices did not boil the less in the bosom of Mr Rock, because he was actually in the land of the Dagos when this story opens; striding furiously up a hill beyond the Mexican border, to the white hotel, fringed with ornamental palms, in which it was supposed that the Potters were staying and that the mysterious Hypatia now held her court. Agar Rock was a good specimen of a Puritan, even to look at; he might even have been a virile Puritan of the seventeenth century, rather than the softer and more sophisticated Puritan of the twentieth. If you had told him that his antiquated black hat and habitual black frown, and fine flinty features, cast a gloom over the sunny land of palms and vines, he would have been very much gratified. He looked to right and left with eyes bright with universal suspicions. And, as he did so, he saw two figures on the ridge above him, outlined against the clear sub-tropical sunset; figures in a momentary posture which might have made even a less suspicious man suspect something.

One of the figures was rather remarkable in itself. It was poised at the exact angle of the turning road above the valley, as if by an instinct for the site as well as the attitude of statuary. It was wrapt in a great black cloak, in the Byronic manner, and the head that rose above it in swarthy beauty was remarkably like Byron's. This man had the same curling hair and curling nostrils; and he seemed to be snorting something of the same scorn and indignation against the world. He grasped in his hand a rather long cane or walking-stick, which having a spike of the sort used for mountaineering, carried at the moment a fanciful suggestion of a spear. It was rendered all the more fanciful by something comically contradictory in the figure of the other man, who carried an umbrella. It was indeed a new and neatly-rolled umbrella, very different, for instance, from Father Brown's umbrella: and he was neatly clad like a clerk in light holiday clothes; a stumpy stoutish bearded man; but the prosaic umbrella was raised and even brandished at an acute angle of attack. The taller man thrust back at him, but in a hasty defensive manner; and then the scene rather collapsed into comedy; for the umbrella opened of itself and its owner almost seemed to sink behind it, while the other man had the air of pushing his spear through a great grotesque shield. But the other man did not push it, or the quarrel, very far; he plucked out the point, turned away impatiently and strode down the road; while the other, rising and carefully refolding his umbrella, turned in the opposite direction towards the hotel. Rock had not heard any of the words of the quarrel, which must have immediately preceded this brief and rather absurd bodily conflict; but as he went up the road in the track of the short man with the beard, he revolved many things. And the romantic cloak and rather operatic good looks of the one man, combined with the sturdy self-assertion of the other, fitted in with the whole story which he had come to seek; and he knew that he could have fixed those two strange figures with their names: Romanes and Potter.

His view was in every way confirmed when he entered the pillared porch; and heard the voice of the bearded man raised high in altercation or command. He was evidently speaking to the manager or staff of the hotel, and Rock heard enough to know that he was warning them of a wild and dangerous character in the neighbourhood.

'If he's really been to the hotel already,' the little man was saying, in answer to some murmur, 'all I can say is that you'd better not let him in again. Your police ought to be looking after a fellow of that sort, but anyhow, I won't have the lady pestered with him.'

Rock listened in grim silence and growing conviction; then he slid across the vestibule to an alcove where he saw the hotel register and turning to the last page, saw 'the fellow' had indeed been to the hotel already. There appeared the name of 'Rudel Romanes,' that romantic public character in very large and florid foreign lettering; and after a space under it, rather close together, the names of Hypatia Potter and Ellis T. Potter, in a correct and quite American handwriting.

Agar Rock looked moodily about him, and saw in the surroundings and even the small decorations of the hotel everything that he hated most. It is perhaps unreasonable to complain of oranges growing on orange-trees, even in small tubs; still more of their only growing on threadbare curtains or faded wallpapers as a formal scheme of ornament. But to him those red and golden moons, decoratively alternated with silver moons, were in a queer way the quintessence of all moonshine. He saw in them all that sentimental deterioration which his principles deplored in modern manners, and which his prejudices vaguely connected with the warmth and softness of the South. It annoyed him even to catch sight of a patch of dark canvas, half-showing a Watteau shepherd with a guitar, or a blue tile with a commonplace design of a Cupid on a dolphin. His common sense would have told him that he might have seen these things in a shopwindow on Fifth Avenue; but where they were, they seemed like a taunting siren voice of the Paganism of the Mediterranean. And then suddenly, the look of all these things seemed to alter, as a still mirror will flicker when a figure has flashed past it for a moment; and he knew the whole room was full of a challenging presence. He turned almost stiffly, and with a sort of resistance, and knew that he was facing the famous Hypatia, of whom he had read and heard for so many years.

Hypatia Potter, *née* Hard, was one of those people to whom the word 'radiant' really does apply definitely and derivatively.

11

That is, she allowed what the papers called her Personality to go out from her in rays. She would have been equally beautiful, and to some tastes more attractive, if she had been self-contained; but she had always been taught to believe that self-containment was only selfishness. She would have said that she had lost Self in Service; it would perhaps be truer to say that she had asserted Self in Service; but she was quite in good faith about the service. Therefore her outstanding starry blue eyes really struck outwards, as in the old metaphor that made eyes like Cupid's darts, killing at a distance; but with an abstract conception of conquest beyond any mere coquetry. Her pale fair hair, though arranged in a saintly halo, had a look of almost electric radiation. And when she understood that the stranger before her was Mr Agar Rock, of the *Minneapolis Meteor*, her eyes took on themselves the range of long searchlights, sweeping the horizon of the States.

But in this the lady was mistaken; as she sometimes was. For Agar Rock was not Agar Rock of the *Minneapolis Meteor*. He was at that moment merely Agar Rock; there had surged up in him a great and sincere moral impulsion, beyond the coarse courage of the interviewer. A feeling profoundly mixed of a chivalrous and national sensibility to beauty, with an instant itch for moral action of some definite sort, which was also national, nerved him to face a great scene; and to deliver a noble insult. He remembered the original Hypatia, the beautiful Neo-Platonist, and how he had been thrilled as a boy by Kingsley's romance in which the young monk denounces her for harlotries and idolatries. He confronted her with an iron gravity and said:

'If you'll pardon me, Madam, I should like to have a word with you in private.'

'Well,' she said, sweeping the room with her splendid gaze, 'I don't know whether you consider this place private.'

Rock also gazed round the room and could see no sign of life less vegetable than the orange trees, except what looked like a large black mushroom, which he recognized as the hat of some native priest or other, stolidly smoking a black local cigar, and otherwise as stagnant as any vegetable. He looked for a moment at the heavy, expressionless features, noting the rudeness of that

12

peasant type from which priests so often come, in Latin and especially Latin-American countries; and lowered his voice a little as he laughed.

'I don't imagine that Mexican padre knows our language,' he said. 'Catch those lumps of laziness learning any language but their own. Oh, I can't swear he's a Mexican; he might be anything; mongrel Indian or nigger, I suppose. But I'll answer for it he's not an American. Our ministries don't produce that debased type.'

'As a matter of fact,' said the debased type, removing his black cigar, 'I'm English and my name is Brown. But pray let me leave you if you wish to be private.'

'If you're English,' said Rock warmly, 'you ought to have some normal Nordic instinct for protesting against all this nonsense. Well, it's enough to say now that I'm in a position to testify that there's a pretty dangerous fellow hanging round this place; a tall fellow in a cloak, like those old pictures of crazy poets.'

'Well, you can't go much by that,' said the priest mildly; 'a lot of people round here use those cloaks, because the chill strikes very suddenly after sunset.'

Rock darted a dark and doubtful glance at him; as if suspecting some evasion in the interests of all that was symbolized to him by mushroom hats and moonshine. 'It wasn't only the cloak,' he growled, 'though it was partly the way he wore it. The whole look of the fellow was theatrical, down to his damned theatrical good looks. And if you'll forgive me, Madam, I strongly advise you to have nothing to do with him, if he comes bothering here. Your husband has already told the hotel people to keep him out –'

Hypatia sprang to her feet and, with a very unusual gesture, covered her face, thrusting her fingers into her hair. She seemed to be shaken, possibly with sobs, but by the time she had recovered they had turned into a sort of wild laughter.

'Oh, you are all too funny,' she said, and, in a way very unusual with her, ducked and darted to the door and disappeared.

'Bit hysterical when they laugh like that,' said Rock uncomfortably; then, rather at a loss, and turning to the little priest: 'as I say, if you're English, you ought really to be on my side against these Dagos, anyhow. Oh, I'm not one of those who talk tosh about Anglo-Saxons; but there is such a thing as history. You can always claim that America got her civilization from England.'

'Also, to temper our pride,' said Father Brown, 'we must always admit that England got her civilization from Dagos.'

Again there glowed in the other's mind the exasperated sense that his interlocutor was fencing with him, and fencing on the wrong side, in some secret and evasive way; and he curtly professed a failure to comprehend.

'Well, there was a Dago, or possibly a Wop, called Julius Caesar,' said Father Brown; 'he was afterwards killed in a stabbing match; you know these Dagos always use knives. And there was another one called Augustine, who brought Christianity to our little island; and really, I don't think we should have had much civilization without those two.'

'Anyhow, that's all ancient history,' said the somewhat irritated journalist, 'and I'm very much interested in modern history. What I see is that these scoundrels are bringing Paganism to our country, and destroying all the Christianity there is. Also destroying all the common sense there is. All settled habits, all solid social order, all the way in which the farmers who were our fathers and grandfathers did manage to live in the world, melted into a hot mush by sensations and sensualities about film-stars who are divorced every month or so, and make every silly girl think that marriage is only a way of getting divorced.'

'You are quite right,' said Father Brown. 'Of course I quite agree with you there. But you must make some allowances. Perhaps these Southern people are a little prone to that sort of fault. You must remember that Northern people have other kinds of faults. Perhaps these surroundings do encourage people to give too rich an importance to mere romance ...'

The whole integral indignation of Agar Rock's life rose up within him at the word.

'I hate Romance,' he said, hitting the little table before him. 'I've fought the papers I worked for for forty years about the infernal trash. Every blackguard bolting with a barmaid is called a romantic elopement or something; and now our own Hypatia

14

Hard, a daughter of decent people, may get dragged into some rotten romantic divorce case, that will be trumpeted to the whole world as happily as a royal wedding. This mad poet Romanes is hanging round her; and you bet the spotlight will follow him, as if he were any rotten little Dago who is called the Great Lover on the films. I saw him outside; and he's got the regular spotlight face. Now my sympathies are with decency and common sense. My sympathies are with poor Potter, a plain straightforward broker from Pittsburg, who thinks he has a right to his own home. And he's making a fight for it, too. I heard him hollering at the management, telling them to keep that rascal out; and quite right too. The people here seem a sly and slinky lot; but I rather fancy he's put the fear of God into them already.'

'As a matter of fact,' said Father Brown, 'I rather agree with you about the manager and the men in this hotel; but you mustn't judge all Mexicans by them. Also I fancy the gentleman you speak of has not only hollered, but handed round dollars enough to get the whole staff on his side. I saw them locking doors and whispering most excitedly. By the way, your plain straightforward friend seems to have a lot of money.'

'I've no doubt his business does well,' said Rock. 'He's quite the best type of sound business man. What do you mean?'

'I fancied it might suggest another thought to you,' said Father Brown; and, rising with rather heavy civility, he left the room.

Rock watched the Potters very carefully that evening at dinner; and gained some new impressions, though none that disturbed his deep sense of the wrong that probably threatened the peace of the Potter home. Potter himself proved worthy of somewhat closer study; though the journalist had at first accepted him as prosaic and unpretentious, there was a pleasure in recognizing finer lines in what he considered the hero or victim of a tragedy. Potter had really rather a thoughtful and distinguished face, though worried and occasionally petulant. Rock got an impression that the man was recovering from an illness; his faded hair was thin but rather long, as if it had been lately neglected, and his rather unusual beard gave the onlooker the same notion.

Certainly he spoke once or twice to his wife in a rather sharp and acid manner, fussing about tablets or some detail of digestive science; but his real worry was doubtless concerned with the danger from without. His wife played up to him in the splendid if somewhat condescending manner of a Patient Griselda; but her eyes also roamed continually to the doors and shutters, as if in half-hearted fear of an invasion. Rock had only too good reason to dread, after her curious outbreak, the fact that her fear might turn out to be only half-hearted.

It was in the middle of that night that the extraordinary event occurred. Rock, imagining himself to be the last to go up to bed, was surprised to find Father Brown still tucked obscurely under an orange-tree in the hall, and placidly reading a book. He returned the other's farewell without further words, and the journalist had his foot on the lowest step of the stair, when suddenly the outer door sprang on its hinges and shook and rattled under the shock of blows planted from without; and a great voice louder than the blows was heard violently demanding admission. Somehow the journalist was certain that the blows had been struck with a pointed stick like an alpenstock. He looked back at the darkened lower floor, and saw the servants of the hotel sliding here and there to see that the doors were locked; and not unlocking them. Then he slowly mounted to his room, and sat down furiously to write his report.

He described the siege of the hotel; the evil atmosphere; the shabby luxury of the place; the shifty evasions of the priest; above all, that terrible voice crying without, like a wolf prowling round the house. Then, as he wrote, he heard a new sound and sat up suddenly. It was a long repeated whistle, and in his mood he hated it doubly, because it was like the signal of a conspirator and like the love-call of a bird. There followed an utter silence, in which he sat rigid; then he rose abruptly; for he had heard yet another noise. It was a faint swish followed by a sharp rap or rattle; and he was almost certain that somebody was throwing something at the window. He walked stiffly downstairs, to the floor which was now dark and deserted; or nearly deserted. For the little priest was still sitting under the orange shrub, lit by a low lamp; and still reading his book.

16

'You seem to be sitting up late,' he said harshly.

'Quite a dissipated character,' said Father Brown, looking up with a broad smile, 'reading *Economics of Usury* at all wild hours of the night.'

'The place is locked up,' said Rock.

'Very thoroughly locked up,' replied the other. 'Your friend with the beard seems to have taken every precaution. By the way, your friend with the beard is a little rattled; I thought he was rather cross at dinner.'

'Natural enough,' growled the other, 'if he thinks savages in this savage place are out to wreck his home life.'

'Wouldn't it be better,' said Father Brown, 'if a man tried to make his home life nice inside, while he was protecting it from the things outside.'

'Oh, I know you will work up all the casuistical excuses,' said the other; 'perhaps he was rather snappy with his wife; but he's got the right on his side. Look here, you seem to me to be rather a deep dog. I believe you know more about this than you say. What the devil is going on in this infernal place? Why are you sitting up all night to see it through?'

'Well,' said Father Brown patiently, 'I rather thought my bedroom might be wanted.'

'Wanted by whom?'

'As a matter of fact, Mrs Potter wanted another room,' explained Father Brown with limpid clearness. 'I gave her mine, because I could open the window. Go and see, if you like.'

'I'll see to something else first,' said Rock grinding his teeth. 'You can play your monkey tricks in this Spanish monkey-house, but I'm still in touch with civilization.' He strode into the telephone-booth and rang up his paper; pouring out the whole tale of the wicked priest who helped the wicked poet. Then he ran upstairs into the priest's room, in which the priest had just lit a short candle, showing the windows beyond wide open.

He was just in time to see a sort of rude-ladder unhooked from the window-sill and rolled up by a laughing gentleman on the lawn below. The laughing gentleman was a tall and swarthy gentleman, and was accompanied by a blonde but equally laughing lady. This time, Mr Rock could not even comfort himself by calling her laughter hysterical. It was too horribly genuine; and rang down the rambling garden-paths as she and her troubadour disappeared into the dark thickets.

Agar Rock turned on his companion a face of final and awful justice: like the Day of Judgement.

'Well, all America is going to hear of this,' he said. 'In plain words, you helped her to bolt with that curly-haired lover.'

'Yes,' said Father Brown, 'I helped her to bolt with that curly-haired lover.'

'You call yourself a minister of Jesus Christ,' cried Rock, 'and you boast of a crime.'

'I have been mixed up with several crimes,' said the priest gently. 'Happily for once this is a story without a crime. This is a simple fire-side idyll; that ends with a glow of domesticity.'

'And ends with a rope-ladder instead of a rope,' said Rock. 'Isn't she a married woman?'

'Oh, yes,' said Father Brown.

'Well, oughtn't she to be with her husband?' demanded Rock.

'She is with her husband,' said Father Brown.

The other was startled into anger. 'You lie,' he said. 'The poor little man is still snoring in bed.'

'You seem to know a lot about his private affairs,' said Father Brown plaintively. 'You could almost write a life of the Man with a Beard. The only thing you don't seem ever to have found out about him is his name.'

'Nonsense,' said Rock. 'His name is in the hotel book.'

'I know it is,' answered the priest, nodding gravely, 'in very large letters; the name of Rudel Romanes. Hypatia Potter, who met him here, put her name boldly under his, when she meant to elope with him; and her husband put his name under that, when he pursued them to this place. He put it very close under hers, by way of protest. Then Romanes (who has pots of money, as a popular misanthrope despising men) bribed the brutes in this hotel to bar and bolt it and keep the lawful husband out. And I, as you truly say, helped him to get in.'

When a man is told something that turns things upside-down; that the tail wags the dog; that the fish has caught the fisherman;

that the earth goes round the moon; he takes some little time before he even asks seriously if it is true. He is still content with the consciousness that it is the opposite of the obvious truth. Rock said at last: 'You don't mean that little fellow is the romantic Rudel we're always reading about; and that curly-haired fellow is Mr Potter of Pittsburgh.'

'Yes,' said Father Brown. 'I knew it the moment I clapped eyes on both of them. But I verified it afterwards.'

Rock ruminated for a time and said at last: 'I supppse it's barely possible you're right. But how did you come to have such a notion, in the face of the facts?'

Father Brown looked rather abashed; subsided into a chair, and stared into vacancy, until a faint smile began to dawn on his round and rather foolish face.

'Well,' he said, 'you see – the truth is, I'm not romantic.'

'I don't know what the devil you are,' said Rock roughly.

'Now *you* are romantic,' said Father Brown helpfully. 'For instance, you see somebody looking poetical, and you assume he is a poet. Do you know what the majority of poets look like? What a wild confusion was created by that coincidence of three good-looking aristocrats at the beginning of the nineteenth century: Byron and Goethe and Shelley! Believe me, in the common way, a man may write: "Beauty has laid her flaming lips on mine," or whatever that chap wrote, without being himself particularly beautiful. Besides, do you realize how *old* a man generally is by the time his fame has filled the world? Watts painted Swinburne with a halo of hair; but Swinburne was bald before most of his last American or Australian admirers had heard of his hyacinthine locks. So was D'Annunzio. As a fact, Romanes still has rather a fine head, as you will see if you look at it closely; he looks like an intellectual man; and he is. Unfortunately, like a good many other intellectual men, he's a fool. He's let himself go to seed with selfishness and fussing about his digestion. So that the ambitious American lady, who thought it would be like soaring to Olympus with the Nine Muses to elope with a poet, found that a day or so of it was about enough for her. So that when her husband came after her, and stormed the place, she was delighted to go back to him.'

19

'But her husband?' queried Rock. 'I am still rather puzzled about her husband.'

'Ah, you've been reading too many of your erotic modern novels,' said Father Brown; and partly closed his eyes in answer to the protesting glare of the other. 'I know a lot of stories start with a wildly beautiful woman wedded to some elderly swine in the stock market. But why? In that, as in most things, modern novels are the very reverse of modern. I don't say it never happens; but it hardly ever happens now except by her own fault. Girls nowadays marry whom they like; especially spoilt girls like Hypatia. And whom do they marry? A beautiful wealthy girl like that would have a ring of admirers; and whom would she choose? The chances are a hundred to one that she'd marry very young and choose the handsomest man she met at a dance or a tennis-party. Well, ordinary business men are sometimes handsome. A young god appeared (called Potter) and she wouldn't care if he was a broker or a burglar. But, given the environment, you will admit it's more likely he would be a broker; also, it's quite likely that he'd be called Potter. You see, you are so incurably romantic that your whole case was founded on the idea that a man looking like a young god, couldn't be called Potter. Believe me, names are not so appropriately distributed.'

'Well,' said the other, after a short pause, 'and what do you suppose happened after that?'

Father Brown got up rather abruptly from the seat in which he had collapsed; the candlelight threw the shadow of his short figure across the wall and ceiling, giving an odd impression that the balance of the room had been altered.

'Ah,' he muttered, 'that's the devil of it. That's the real devil. Much worse than the old Indian demons in this jungle. You thought I was only making out a case for the loose ways of these Latin Americans – well, the queer thing about you' – and he blinked owlishly at the other through his spectacles – 'the queerest thing about you is that in a way you're right.

'You say down with romance. I say I'd take my chance in fighting the genuine romances – all the more because they are precious few, outside the first fiery days of youth. I say – take away the Intellectual Friendships; take away the Platonic

Unions; take away the Higher Laws of Self-Fulfilment and the rest, and I'll risk the normal dangers of the job. Take away the love that isn't love, but only pride and vainglory and publicity and making a splash; and we'll take our chance of fighting the love that is love, when it has to be fought, as well as the love that is lust and lechery. Priests know young people will have passions, as doctors know they will have measles. But Hypatia Potter is forty if she is a day, and she cares no more for that little poet than if he were her publisher or her publicity man. That's just the point – he was her publicity man. It's your newspapers that have ruined her; it's living in the limelight; it's wanting to see herself in the headlines, even in a scandal if it were only sufficiently psychic and superior. It's wanting to be George Sand, her name immortally linked with Alfred de Musset. When her real romance of youth was over, it was the sin of middle age that got hold of her; the sin of intellectual ambition. She hasn't got any intellect to speak of; but you don't need any intellect to be an intellectual.'

'I should say she was pretty brainy in one sense,' observed Rock reflectively.

'Yes, in one sense,' said Father Brown. 'In only one sense. In a business sense. Not in any sense that has anything to do with these poor lounging Dagos down here. You curse the Film Stars and tell me you hate romance. Do you suppose the Film Star, who is married for the fifth time, is misled by any romance? Such people are very practical; more practical than you are. You say you admire the simple solid Business Man. Do you suppose that Rudel Romanes isn't a Business Man? Can't you see he knew, quite as well as she did, the advertising advantages of this last grand affair with a famous beauty. He also knew very well that his hold on it was pretty insecure; hence his fussing about and bribing servants to lock doors. But what I mean to say, first and last, is that there'd be a lot less scandal if people didn't idealize sin and pose as sinners. These poor Mexicans may seem sometimes to live like beasts, or rather sin like men; but they don't go in for Ideals. You must at least give them credit for that.'

He sat down again, as abruptly as he had risen, and laughed apologetically. 'Well, Mr Rock,' he said, 'that is my complete confession; the whole horrible story of how I helped a romantic elopement. You can do what you like with it.'

'In that case,' said Rock, rising, 'I will go to my room and make a few alterations in my report. But, first of all, I must ring up my paper and tell them I've been telling them a pack of lies.'

Not much more than half an hour had passed, between the time when Rock had telephoned to say the priest was helping the poet to run away with the lady, and the time when he telephoned to say that the priest had prevented the poet from doing precisely the same thing. But in that short interval of time was born and enlarged and scattered upon the winds the Scandal of Father Brown. The truth is still half an hour behind the slander; and nobody can be certain when or where it will catch up with it. The garrulity of pressmen and the eagerness of enemies had spread the first story through the city, even before it appeared in the first printed version. It was instantly corrected and contradicted by Rock himself, in a second message stating how the story had really ended; but it was by no means certain that the first story was killed. A positively incredible number of people seemed to have read the first issue of the paper and not the second. Again and again, in every corner of the world, like a flame bursting from blackened ashes, there would appear the old tale of the Brown Scandal, or Priest Ruins Potter Home. Tireless apologists of the priest's party watched for it, and patiently tagged after it with contradictions and exposures and letters of protest. Sometimes the letters were published in the papers; and sometimes they were not. But still nobody knew how many people had heard the story without hearing the contradiction. It was possible to find whole blocks of blameless and innocent people who thought the Mexican Scandal was an ordinary recorded historical incident like the Gunpowder Plot. Then somebody would enlighten these simple people, only to discover that the old story had started afresh among a few quite educated people, who would seem the last people on earth to be duped by it. And so the two Father Browns chase each other round the world for ever; the first a shameless criminal fleeing from justice; the second a martyr broken by slander, in a halo of rehabilitation. But neither of them is very like the real Father Brown, who is not broken at all; but goes stumping with his stout umbrella through life, liking most of the people in it; accepting the world as his companion, but never as his judge.

TWO

The Quick One

THE strange story of the incongruous strangers is still remembered
along that strip of the Sussex coast, where the large and quiet
hotel called the Maypole and Garland looks across its own gardens to the sea. Two quaintly assorted figures did, indeed, enter
that quiet hotel on that sunny afternoon; one being conspicuous
in the sunlight, and visible over the whole shore, by the fact
of wearing a lustrous green turban, surrounding a brown face
and a black beard; the other would have seemed to some even
more wild and weird, by reason of his wearing a soft black clergyman's hat with a yellow moustache and yellow hair of leonine
length. He at least had often been seen preaching on the sands
or conducting Band of Hope services with a little wooden spade;
only he had certainly never been seen going into the bar of an
hotel. The arrival of these quaint companions was the climax
of the story, but not the beginning of it; and, in order to make
a rather mysterious story as clear as possible, it is better to begin
at the beginning.

Half an hour before those two conspicuous figures entered the
hotel, and were noticed by everybody, two other very inconspicuous figures had also entered it, and been noticed by nobody.
One was a large man, and handsome in a heavy style, but he had
a knack of taking up very little room, like a background;
only an almost morbidly suspicious examination of his boots
would have told anybody that he was an Inspector of Police
in plain clothes; in very plain clothes. The other was a drab and
insignificant little man, also in plain clothes, only that they
happened to be clerical clothes; but nobody had ever seen *him*
preaching on the sands.

These travellers also found themselves in a sort of large
smoking-room with a bar, for a reason which determined all the

24

events of that tragic afternoon. The truth is that the respectable hotel called the Maypole and Garlard was being 'done-up'. Those who had liked it in the past were moved to say that it was being done down; or possibly done in. This was the opinion of the local grumbler, Mr Raggley, the eccentric old gentleman who drank cherry brandy in a corner and cursed. Anyhow, it was being carefully stripped of all the stray indications that it had once been an English inn; and being busily turned, yard by yard and room by room, into something resembling the sham palace of a Levantine usurer in an American film. It was, in short, being 'decorated'; but the only part where the decoration was complete, and where customers could yet be made comfortable, was this large room leading out of the hall. It had once been honourably known as a Bar Parlour and was now mysteriously known as a Saloon Lounge, and was newly 'decorated', in the manner of an Asiatic Divan. For Oriental ornament pervaded the new scheme; and where there had once been a gun hung on hooks, and sporting prints and a stuffed fish in a glass case, there were now festoons of Eastern drapery and trophies of scimitars, tulwards and yataghans, as if in unconscious preparation for the coming of the gentleman with the turban. The practical point was, however, that the few guests who did arrive had to be shepherded into this lounge, now swept and garnished, because all the more regular and refined parts of the hotel were still in a state of transition. Perhaps that was also the reason why even those few guests were somewhat neglected, the manager and others being occupied with explanations or exhortations elsewhere. Anyhow, the first two travellers who arrived had to kick their heels for some time unattended.

The bar was at the moment entirely empty, and the Inspector rang and rapped impatiently on the counter; but the little clergyman had already dropped into a lounge seat and seemed in no hurry for anything. Indeed his friend the policeman, turning his head, saw that the round face of the little cleric had gone quite blank, as it had a way of doing sometimes; he seemed to be staring through his moonlike spectacles at the newly decorated wall.

'I may as well offer you a penny for your thoughts,' said

Inspector Greenwood, turning from the counter with a sigh, 'as nobody seems to want my pennies for anything else. This seems to be the only room in the house that isn't full of ladders and whitewash; and this is so empty that there isn't even a potboy to give me a pot of beer.'

'Oh ... my thoughts are not worth a penny, let alone a pot of beer,' answered the cleric, wiping his spectacles, 'I don't know why ... but I was thinking how easy it would be to commit a murder here.'

'It's all very well for you, Father Brown,' said the Inspector good-humouredly. 'You've had a lot more murders than your fair share; and we poor policemen sit starving all our lives, even for a little one. But why should you say ... Oh I see, you're looking at all those Turkish daggers on the wall. There are plenty of things to commit a murder *with*, if that's what you mean. But not more than there are in any ordinary kitchen: carving-knives or pokers or what not. That isn't where the snag of a murder comes in.'

Father Brown seemed to recall his rambling thoughts in some bewilderment; and said that he supposed so.

'Murder is always easy,' said Inspector Greenwood. 'There can't possibly be anything more easy than murder. I could murder you at this minute – more easily than I can get a drink in this damned bar. The only difficulty is committing a murder without committing oneself as a murderer. It's this shyness about owning up to a murder; it's this silly modesty of murderers about their own masterpieces, that makes the trouble. They will stick to this extraordinary fixed idea of killing people without being found out; and that's what restrains them, even in a room full of daggers. Otherwise every cutler's shop would be piled with corpses. And that, by the way, explains the one kind of murder that really *can't* be prevented. Which is why, of course, we poor bobbies are always blamed for not preventing it. When a madman murders a King or a President, it can't be prevented. You can't make a King live in a coal-cellar, or carry about a President in a steel box. Anybody can murder him who does not mind being a murderer. That is where the madman is like the martyr –

sort of beyond this world. A real fanatic can always kill anybody he likes.'

Before the priest could reply, a joyous band of bagmen rolled into the room like a shoal of porpoises; and the magnificent bellow of a big, beaming man, with an equally big and beaming tie-pin, brought the eager and obsequious manager running like a dog to the whistle, with a rapidity which the police in plain clothes had failed to inspire.

'I'm sure I'm very sorry, Mr Jukes,' said the manager, who wore a rather agitated smile and a wave or curl of very varnished hair across his forehead. 'We're rather understaffed at present; and I had to attend to something in the hotel, Mr Jukes.'

Mr Jukes was magnanimous, but in a noisy way; and ordered drinks all round, conceding one even to the almost cringing manager. Mr Jukes was a traveller for a very famous and fashionable wine and spirits firm; and may have conceived himself as lawfully the leader in such a place. Anyhow, he began a boisterous monologue, rather tending to tell the manager how to manage his hotel; and the others seemed to accept him as an authority. The policeman and the priest had retired to a low bench and small table in the background, from which they watched events, up to that rather remarkable moment when the policeman had very decisively to intervene.

For the next thing that happened, as already narrated, was the astonishing apparition of a brown Asiatic in a green turban, accompanied by the (if possible) more astonishing apparition of a Noncomformist minister; omens such as appear before a doom. In this case there was no doubt about evidence for the portent. A taciturn but observant boy cleaning the steps for the last hour (being a leisurely worker), the dark, fat, bulky bar-attendant, even the diplomatic but distracted manager, all bore witness to the miracle.

The apparitions, as the sceptics say, were due to perfectly natural causes. The man with the mane of yellow hair and the semi-clerical clothes was not only familiar as a preacher on the sands, but as a propagandist throughout the modern world. He was no less a person than the Rev. David Pryce-Jones, whose far-resounding slogan was Prohibition and Purification for Our Land and the Britains Overseas. He was an excellent public speaker and organizer; and an idea had occurred to him that ought to have occurred to Prohibitionists long ago. It was the simple idea that, if Prohibition is right, some honour is due to the Prophet who was perhaps the first Prohibitionist. He had corresponded with the leaders of Mahommedan religious thought, and had finally induced a distinguished Moslem (one of whose names was Akbar and the rest an untranslatable ululation of Allah with attributes) to come and lecture in England on the ancient Moslem veto on wine. Neither of them certainly had been in a public-house bar before; but they had come there by the process already described; driven from the genteel tea-rooms, shepherded into the newly-decorated saloon. Probably all would have been well, if the great Prohibitionist, in his innocence, had not advanced to the counter and asked for a glass of milk.

The commercial travellers, though a kindly race, emitted involuntary noises of pain; a murmur of suppressed jests was heard, as 'Shun the bowl,' or 'Better bring out the cow'. But the magnificent Mr Jukes, feeling it due to his wealth and tie-pin to produce more refined humour, fanned himself as one about to faint, and said pathetically: 'They know they can knock me down with a feather. They know a breath will blow me away. They know my doctor says I'm not to have these shocks. And they come and drink cold milk in cold blood, before my very eyes.'

The Rev. David Pryce-Jones, accustomed to deal with hecklers at public meetings, was so unwise as to venture on remonstrance and recrimination, in this very different and much more popular atmosphere. The Oriental total abstainer abstained from speech as well as spirits; and certainly gained in dignity by doing so. In fact, so far as he was concerned, the Moslem culture certainly scored a silent victory; he was obviously so much more of a gentleman than the commercial gentlemen, that a faint irritation began to arise against his aristocratic aloofness; and when Mr Pryce-Jones began to refer in argument to something of the kind, the tension became very acute indeed.

'I ask you, friends,' said Mr Pryce-Jones, with expansive platform gestures, 'why does our friend here set an example to us Christians in truly Christian self-control and brotherhood? Why does he stand here as a model of true Christianity, of real refinement, of genuine gentlemanly behaviour, amid all the quarrels and riots of such places as these? Because, whatever the doctrinal differences between us, at least in his soil the evil plant, the accursed hop or vine, has never – '

At this crucial moment of the controversy it was that John Raggley, the stormy petrel of a hundred storms of controversy, red-faced, white-haired, his antiquated top-hat on the back of his head, his stick swinging like a club, entered the house like an invading army.

John Raggley was generally regarded as a crank. He was the sort of man who writes letters to the newspaper, which generally do not appear in the newspaper; but which do appear afterwards as pamplets, printed (or misprinted) at his own expense; and circulated to a hundred waste-paper baskets. He had quarrelled alike with the Tory squires and the Radical County Councils; he hated Jews; and he distrusted nearly everything that is sold in shops, or even in hotels. But there was a backing of facts behind his fads; he knew the county in every corner and curious detail; and he was a sharp observer. Even the manager, a Mr Wills, had a shadowy respect for Mr Raggley, having a nose for the sort of lunacy allowed in the gentry; not indeed the prostrate reverence which he had for the jovial magnificence of Mr Jukes, who was really good for trade, but at least a disposition to avoid quarrelling with the old grumbler, partly perhaps out of fear of the old grumbler's tongue.

'And you will have your usual, Sir,' said Mr Wills, leaning and leering across the counter.

'It's the only decent stuff you've still got,' snorted Mr Raggley, slapping down his queer and antiquated hat. 'Damn it, I sometimes think the only English thing left in England is cherry brandy. Cherry brandy does taste of cherries. Can you find me any beer that tastes of hops, or any cider that tastes of apples, or any wine that has the remotest indication of being made out of grapes? There's an infernal swindle going on now in every inn

29

in the country, that would have raised a revolution in any other country. I've found out a thing or two about it, I can tell you. You wait till I can get it printed, and people will sit up. If I could stop our people being poisoned with all this bad drink – '

Here again the Rev. David Pryce-Jones showed a certain failure in tact; though it was a virtue he almost worshipped. He was so unwise as to attempt to establish an alliance with Mr Raggley, by a fine confusion between the idea of bad drink and the idea that drink is bad. Once more he endeavoured to drag his stiff and stately Eastern friend into the argument, as a refined foreigner superior to our rough English ways. He was even so foolish as to talk of a broad theological outlook; and ultimately to mention the name of Mahomet, which was echoed in a sort of explosion.

'God damn your soul!' roared Mr Raggley, with a less broad theological outlook. 'Do you mean that Englishmen mustn't drink English beer, because wine was forbidden in a damned desert by that dirty old humbug Mahomet?'

In an instant the Inspector of Police had reached the middle of the room with a stride. For, the instant before that, a remarkable change had taken place in the demeanour of the Oriental gentleman, who had hitherto stood perfectly still, with steady and shining eyes. He now proceeded, as his friend had said, to set an example in truly Christian self-control and brotherhood by reaching the wall with the bound of a tiger, tearing down one of the heavy knives hanging there and sending it smack like a stone from a sling, so that it stuck quivering in the wall exactly half an inch above Mr Raggley's ear. It would undoubtedly have stuck quivering in Mr Raggley, if Inspector Greenwood had not been just in time to jerk the arm and deflect the aim. Father Brown continued in his seat, watching the scene with screwed-up eyes and a screw of something almost like a smile at the corners of his mouth, as if he saw something beyond the mere momentary violence of the quarrel.

And then the quarrel took a curious turn; which may not be understood by everybody, until men like Mr John Raggley are better understood than they are. For the red-faced old fanatic was standing up and laughing uproariously as if it were the best joke he had ever heard. All his snapping vituperation and bitterness seemed to have gone out of him; and he regarded the other fanatic, who had just tried to murder him, with a sort of boisterous benevolence.

'Blast your eyes,' he said, 'you're the first man I've met in twenty years!'

'Do you charge this man, Sir?' said the Inspector, looking doubtful.

'Charge him, of course not,' said Raggley. 'I'd stand him a drink if he were allowed any drinks. I hadn't any business to insult his religion; and I wish to God all you skunks had the guts to kill a man, I won't say for insulting your religion, because you haven't got any, but for insulting anything – even your beer.'

'Now he's called us all skunks,' said Father Brown to Greenwood, 'peace and harmony seem to be restored. I wish that teetotal lecturer could get himself impaled on his friend's knife; it was he who made all the mischief.'

As he spoke, the odd groups in the room were already beginning to break up; it had been found possible to clear the commercial room for the commercial travellers, and they adjourned to it, the potboy carrying a new round of drinks after them on a tray. Father Brown stood for a moment gazing at the glasses left on the counter; recognizing at once the ill-omened glass of milk, and another which smelt of whisky; and then turned just in time to see the parting between those two quaint figures, fanatics of the East and West. Raggley was still ferociously genial; there was still something a little darkling and sinister about the Moslem, which was perhaps natural; but he bowed himself out with grave gestures of dignified reconciliation; and there was every indication that the trouble was really over.

Some importance, however, continued attached, in the mind of Father Brown at least, to the memory and interpretation of those last courteous salutes between the combatants. Because curiously enough, when Father Brown came down very early next morning, to perform his religious duties in the neighbourhood, he found the long saloon bar, with its fantastic Asiatic decoration, filled with a dead white light of daybreak in which every detail was distinct; and one of the details was the dead body of John Raggley bent and crushed into a corner of the room, with the heavy-hilted crooked dagger rammed through his heart.

Father Brown went very softly upstairs again and summoned his friend the Inspector; and the two stood beside the corpse, in a house in which no one else was as yet stirring.

'We mustn't either assume or avoid the obvious,' said Greenwood after a silence, 'but it is well to remember, I think, what I was saying to you yesterday afternoon. It's rather odd, by the way, that I should have said it – yesterday afternoon.'

'I know,' said the priest, nodding with an owlish stare.

'I said,' observed Greenwood, 'that the one sort of murder we can't stop is murder by somebody like a religious fanatic. That brown fellow probably thinks that if he's hanged, he'll go straight to Paradise for defending the honour of the Prophet.'

'There is that, of course,' said Father Brown. 'It would be very reasonable, so to speak, of our Moslem friend to have stabbed him. And you may say we don't know of anybody else yet, who could at all reasonably have stabbed him. But ... but I was thinking ...' And his round face suddenly went blank again and all speech died on his lips.

'What's the matter now?' asked the other.

'Well, I know it sounds funny,' said Father Brown in a forlorn voice. 'But I was thinking ... I was thinking, in a way, it doesn't much matter who stabbed him.'

'Is this the New Morality?' asked his friend. 'Or the old Casuistry, perhaps. Are the Jesuits really going in for murder?'

'I didn't say it didn't matter who murdered him,' said Father Brown. 'Of course the man who stabbed him might possibly be the man who murdered him. But it might be quite a different man. Anyhow, it was done at quite a different time. I suppose you'll want to work on the hilt for finger-prints; but don't take too much notice of them. I can imagine other reasons for other people sticking this knife in the poor old boy. Not very edifying reasons, of course, but quite distinct from the murder. You'll have to put some more knives into him, before you find out about that.'

'You mean – ' began the other, watching him keenly.

'I mean the autopsy,' said the priest, 'to find the real cause of death.'

'You're quite right, I believe,' said the Inspector, 'about the stabbing, anyhow. We must wait for the doctor; but I'm pretty sure he'll say you're right. There isn't blood enough. This knife was stuck in the corpse when it had been cold for hours. But why?'

'Possibly to put the blame on the Mahommedan,' answered Father Brown. 'Pretty mean, I admit, but not necessarily murder. I fancy there are people in this place trying to keep secrets, who are not necessarily the murderers.'

'I haven't speculated on that line yet,' said Greenwood. 'What makes you think so?'

'What I said yesterday, when we first came into this horrible room. I said it would be easy to commit a murder here. But I wasn't thinking about all those stupid weapons, though you thought I was. About something quite different.'

For the next few hours the Inspector and his friend conducted a close and thorough investigation into the goings and comings of everybody for the last twenty-four hours, the way the drinks had been distributed, the glasses that were washed or unwashed, and every detail about every individual involved, or apparently not involved. One might have supposed they thought that thirty people had been poisoned, as well as one.

It seemed certain that nobody had entered the building except by the big entrance that adjoined the bar; all the others were blocked in one way or another by the repairs. A boy had been cleaning the steps outside this entrance; but he had nothing very clear to report. Until the amazing entry of the Turk in the Turban, with his teetotal lecturer, there did not seem to have been much custom of any kind, except for the commercial travellers who came in to take what they called 'quick ones'; and they seemed to have moved together, like Wordsworth's Cloud; there was a slight difference of opinion between the boy outside and the men inside about whether one of them had not been abnormally quick in obtaining a quick one, and come out on the doorstep by himself; but the manager and the barman had no

memory of any such independent individual. The manager
and the barman knew all the travellers quite well, and there was
no doubt about their movements as a whole. They had stood at
the bar chaffing and drinking; they had been involved, through
their lordly leader, Mr Jukes, in a not very serious altercation
with Mr Pryce-Jones; and they had witnessed the sudden and
very serious altercation between Mr Akbar and Mr Raggley.
Then they were told they could adjourn to the Commercial
Room, and did so, their drinks being borne after them like a
trophy.

'There's precious little to go on,' said Inspector Greenwood.
'Of course a lot of officious servants must do their duty as usual,
and wash out all the glasses; including old Raggley's glass. If it
weren't for everybody else's efficiency, we detectives might be
quite efficient.'

'I know,' said Father Brown, and his mouth took on again the
twisted smile. 'I sometimes think criminals invented hygiene.
Or perhaps hygienic reformers invented crime; they look like it,
some of them. Everybody talks about foul dens and filthy slums
in which crime can run riot; but it's just the other way. They are
called foul, not because crimes are committed, but because crimes
are discovered. It's in the neat, spotless, clean and tidy places
that crime can run riot; no mud to make footprints; no dregs
to contain poison; kind servants washing out all traces of the
murder; and the murderer killing and cremating six wives and
all for want of a little Christian dirt. Perhaps I express myself with
too much warmth – but look here. As it happens, I do remember
one glass, which has doubtless been cleaned since, but I should
like to know more about it.'

'Do you mean Raggley's glass?' asked Greenwood.

'No; I mean Nobody's glass,' replied the priest. 'It stood near
that glass of milk and it still held an inch or two of whisky. Well,
you and I had no whisky. I happen to remember that the manager, when treated by the jovial Jukes, had "a drop of gin". I
hope you don't suggest that our Moslem was a whisky-drinker
disguised in a green turban; or that the Rev. David Pryce-Jones
managed to drink whisky and milk together, without noticing
it.'

'Most of the commercial travellers took whisky,' said the Inspector. 'They generally do.'

'Yes; and they generally see they get it too,' answered Father Brown. 'In this case, they had it all carefully carted after them to their own room. But this glass was left behind.'

'An accident, I suppose,' said Greenwood doubtfully. 'The man could easily get another in the Commercial Room afterwards.'

Father Brown shook his head. 'You've got to see people as they are. Now these sort of men – well, some call them vulgar and some common; but that's all likes and dislikes. I'd be content to say that they are mostly simple men. Lots of them very good men, very glad to go back to the missus and the kids; some of them might be blackguards; might have had several missuses; or even murdered several missuses. But most of them are simple men; and, mark you, just the least tiny little bit drunk. Not much; there's many a duke or don at Oxford drunker; but when that sort of man is at that stage of conviviality, he simply can't help noticing things, and noticing them very loud. Don't you observe that the least little incident jerks them into speech; if the beer froths over, they froth over with it, and have to say, "Whoa, Emma," or, "Doing me proud, aren't you?" Now I should say it's flatly impossible for five of these festive beings to sit round a table in the Commercial Room, and have only four glasses set before them, the fifth man being left out, without making a shout about it. Probably they would all make a shout about it. Certainly *he* would make a shout about it. He wouldn't wait, like an Englishman of another class, till he could get a drink quietly later. The air would resound with things like, "And what about little me?" or, "Here, George, have I joined the Band of Hope?" or, "Do you see any green in my turban, George?" But the barman heard no such complaints. I take it as certain that the glass of whisky left behind had been nearly emptied by somebody else; somebody we haven't thought about yet.'

'But can you think of any such person?' asked the other.

'It's because the manager and the barman won't hear of any such person, that you dismiss the one really independent piece of evidence; the evidence of that boy outside cleaning the steps.

He says that a man, who well may have been a bagman, but who did not, in fact, stick to the other bagmen, went in and came out again almost immediately. The manager and the barman never saw him; or say they never saw him. But he got a glass of whisky from the bar somehow. Let us call him, for the sake of argument, The Quick One. Now you know I don't often interfere with your business, which I know you do better than I should do it, or should want to do it. I've never had anything to do with setting police machinery at work, or running down criminals, or anything like that. But, for the first time in my life, I want to do it now. I want you to find The Quick One; to follow The Quick One to the ends of the earth; to set the whole infernal official machinery at work like a drag-net across the nations, and jolly well recapture The Quick One. Because he is the man we want.'

Greenwood made a despairing gesture. 'Has he face or form or any visible quality except quickness?' he inquired.

'He was wearing a sort of Inverness cape,' said Father Brown, 'and he told the boy outside he must reach Edinburgh by next morning. That's all the boy outside remembers. But I know your organization has got on to people with less clue than that.'

'You seem very keen on this,' said the Inspector, a little puzzled.

The priest looked puzzled also, as if at his own thoughts; he sat with knotted brow and then said abruptly:

'You see, it's so easy to be misunderstood. All men matter. You matter. I matter. It's the hardest thing in theology to believe.'

The Inspector stared at him without comprehension; but he proceeded.

'We matter to God – God only knows why. But that's the only possible justification of the existence of policemen.' The policeman did not seem enlightened as to his own cosmic justification. 'Don't you see, the law really is right in a way, after all. If all men matter, all murders matter. That which He has so mysteriously created, we must not suffer to be mysteriously destroyed. But – '

He said the last word sharply, like one taking a new step in decision.

'*But*, when once I step off that mystical level of equality, I don't see that most of your important murders are particularly important. You are always telling me that this case and that is important. As a plain, practical man of the world, I must realize that it is the Prime Minister who has been murdered. As a plain, practical man of the world, I don't think that the Prime Minister matters at all. As a mere matter of human importance, I should say he hardly exists at all. Do you suppose if he and the other public men were shot dead tomorrow, there wouldn't be other people to stand up and say that every avenue was being explored, or that the Government had the matter under the gravest consideration? The masters of the modern world don't matter. Even the real masters don't matter much. Hardly anybody you ever read about in a newspaper matters at all.'

He stood up, giving the table a small rap: one of his rare gestures; and his voice changed again.

'But Raggley did matter. He was one of a great line of some half a dozen men who might have saved England. They stand up stark and dark like disregarded sign-posts, down all that smooth descending road which has ended in this swamp of merely commercial collapse. Dean Swift and Dr Johnson and old William Cobbett; they had all without exception the name of being surly or savage, and they were all loved by their friends, and they all deserved to be. Didn't you see how that old man, with the heart of a lion, stood up and forgave his enemy as only fighters can forgive? He jolly well *did* do what that temperance lecturer talked about; he set an example to us Christians and was a model of Christianity. And when there is foul and secret murder of a man like that – then I do think it matters, matters so much that even the modern machinery of police will be a thing that any respectable person may make use of ... Oh, don't mention it. And so, for once in a way, I really do want to make use of you.'

And so, for some stretch of those strange days and nights, we might almost say that the little figure of Father Brown drove before him into action all the armies and engines of the police forces of the Crown, as the little figure of Napoleon drove the batteries and the battle-lines of the vast strategy that covered

Europe. Police stations and post offices worked all night; traffic was stopped, correspondence was intercepted, inquiries were made in a hundred places, in order to track the flying trail of that ghostly figure, without face or name, with an Inverness cape and an Edinburgh ticket.

Meanwhile, of course, the other lines of investigation were not neglected. The full report of the post-mortem had not yet come in; but everybody seemed certain that it was a case of poisoning. This naturally threw the primary suspicion upon the cherry brandy; and this again naturally threw the primary suspicion on the hotel.

'Most probably on the manager of the hotel,' said Greenwood gruffly. 'He looks a nasty little worm to me. Of course it might be something to do with some servant, like the barman; he seems rather a sulky specimen, and Raggley might have cursed him a bit, having a flaming temper, though he was generally generous enough afterwards. But, after all, as I say, the primary responsibility, and therefore the primary suspicion, rests on the manager.'

'Oh, I knew the primary suspicion would rest on the manager,' said Father Brown. 'That was why I didn't suspect him. You see, I rather fancied somebody else must have known that the primary suspicion would rest on the manager; or the servants of the hotel. That is why I said it would be easy to kill anybody in the hotel . . . But you'd better go and have it out with him, I suppose.'

The Inspector went; but came back again after a surprisingly short interview, and found his clerical friend turning over some papers that seemed to be a sort of *dossier* of the stormy career of John Raggley.

'This is a rum go,' said the Inspector. 'I thought I should spend hours cross-examining that slippery little toad there, for we haven't legally got a thing against him. And instead of that, he went to pieces all at once, and I really think he's told me all he knows in sheer funk.'

'I know,' said Father Brown. 'That's the way he went to pieces when he found Raggley's corpse apparently poisoned in his hotel. That's why he lost his head enough to do such a clumsy thing as decorate the corpse with a Turkish knife, to put the blame on the nigger, as he would say. There never is anything the matter with him but funk; he's the very last man that ever would really stick a knife into a live person. I bet he had to nerve himself to stick it into a dead one. But he's the very first person to be frightened of being charged with what he didn't do; and to make a fool of himself, as he did.'

'I suppose I must see the barman too,' observed Greenwood.

'I suppose so,' answered the other. 'I don't believe myself it was any of the hotel people – well, because it was made to look as if it *must* be the hotel people ... But look here, have you seen any of this stuff they've got together about Raggley? He had a jolly interesting life; I wonder whether anyone will write his biography.'

'I took a note of everything likely to affect an affair like this,' answered the official. 'He was a widower; but he did once have a row with a man about his wife; a Scotch land-agent then in these parts; and Raggley seems to have been pretty violent. They say he hated Scotchmen; perhaps that's the reason ... Oh, I know what you are smiling grimly about. A Scotchman ... Perhaps an Edinburgh man.'

'Perhaps,' said Father Brown. 'It's quite likely, though, that he did dislike Scotchmen, apart from private reasons. It's an odd thing, but all that tribe of Tory Radicals, or whatever you call them, who resisted the Whig mercantile movement, all of them did dislike Scotchmen. Cobbett did; Dr Johnson did; Swift described their accent in one of his deadliest passages; even Shakespeare has been accused of the prejudice. But the prejudices of great men generally have something to do with principles. And there was a reason, I fancy. The Scot came from a poor agricultural land, that became a rich industrial land. He was able and active; he thought he was bringing industrial civilization from the north; he simply didn't know that there had been for centuries a rural civilization in the south. His own grandfather's land was highly rural but not civilized ... Well, well, I suppose we can only wait for more news.'

'I hardly think you'll get the latest news out of Shakespeare and Dr Johnson,' grinned the police officer. 'What Shakespeare thought of Scotchmen isn't exactly evidence.'

THE SCANDAL OF FATHER BROWN

Father Brown cocked an eyebrow, as if a new thought had surprised him. 'Why, now I come to think of it,' he said, 'there might be better evidence, even out of Shakespeare. He doesn't often mention Scotchmen. But he was rather fond of making fun of Welshmen.'

The Inspector was searching his friend's face; for he fancied he recognized an alertness behind its demure expression.

'By Jove,' he said. 'Nobody thought of turning the suspicions *that* way, anyhow.'

'Well,' said Father Brown, with broad-minded calm, 'you started by talking about fanatics; and how a fanatic could do anything. Well, I suppose we had the honour of entertaining in this bar-parlour yesterday, about the biggest and loudest and most fat-headed fanatic in the modern world. If being a pig-headed idiot with one idea is the way to murder, I put in a claim for my reverend brother Pryce-Jones, the Prohibitionist, in preference to all the fakirs in Asia, and it's perfectly true, as I told you, that his horrible glass of milk was standing side by side on the counter with the mysterious glass of whisky.'

'Which you think was mixed up with the murder,' said Greenwood, staring. 'Look here, I don't know whether you're really serious or not.'

Even as he was looking steadily in his friend's face, finding something still inscrutable in its expression, the telephone rang stridently behind the bar. Lifting the flap in the counter Inspector Greenwood passed rapidly inside, unhooked the receiver, listened for an instant, and then uttered a shout; not addressed to his interlocutor, but to the universe in general. Then he listened still more attentively and said explosively at intervals, 'Yes, yes ... Come round at once; bring him round if possible ... Good piece of work ... Congratulate you.'

Then Inspector Greenwood came back into the outer lounge, like a man who has renewed his youth, sat down squarely on his seat, with his hands planted on his knees, stared at his friend, and said:

'Father Brown, I don't know how you do it. You seem to have known he was a murderer before anybody else knew he was a man. He was nobody; he was nothing; he was a slight confusion

40

in the evidence; nobody in the hotel saw him; the boy on the steps could hardly swear to him; he was just a fine shade of doubt founded on an extra dirty glass. But we've got him, and he's the man we want.'

Father Brown had risen with the sense of the crisis, mechanically clutching the papers destined to be so valuable to the biographer of Mr Raggley; and stood staring at his friend. Perhaps this gesture jerked his friend's mind to fresh confirmations.

'Yes, we've got The Quick One. And very quick he was, like quicksilver, in making his get-away; we only just stopped him – off on a fishing trip to Orkney, he said. But he's the man, all right; he's the Scotch land-agent who made love to Raggley's wife; he's the man who drank Scotch whisky in this bar and then took a train for Edinburgh. And nobody would have known it but for you.'

'Well, what I meant,' began Father Brown, in a rather dazed tone; and at that instant there was a rattle and rumble of heavy vehicles outside the hotel; and two or three other and subordinate policemen blocked the bar with their presence. One of them, invited by his superior to sit down, did so in an expansive manner, like one at once happy and fatigued; and he also regarded Father Brown with admiring eyes.

'Got the murderer, Sir, oh yes,' he said: 'I know he's a murderer, 'cause he bally nearly murdered me. I've captured some tough characters before now; but never one like this – hit me in the stomach like the kick of a horse and nearly got away from five men. Oh, you've got a real killer this time, Inspector.'

'Where is he?' asked Father Brown, staring.

'Outside in the van, in handcuffs,' replied the policeman, 'and, if you're wise, you'll leave him there – for the present.'

Father Brown sank into a chair in a sort of soft collapse; and the papers he had been nervously clutching were shed around him, shooting and sliding about the floor like sheets of breaking snow. Not only his face, but his whole body, conveyed the impression of a punctured balloon.

'Oh ... Oh,' he repeated, as if any further oath would be inadequate. 'Oh ... I've done it again.'

'If you mean you've caught the criminal again,' began Greenwood. But his friend stopped him with a feeble explosion, like that of expiring soda-water.

'I mean,' said Father Brown, 'that it's always happening; and really, I don't know why. I always try to say what I mean. But everybody else means such a lot by what I say.'

'What in the world is the matter now?' cried Greenwood, suddenly exasperated.

'Well, I say things,' said Father Brown in a weak voice, which could alone convey the weakness of the words. 'I say things, but everybody seems to know they mean more than they say. Once I saw a broken mirror and said "Something has happened" and they all answered, "Yes, yes, as you truly say, two men wrestled and one ran into the garden," and so on. I don't understand it, "Something happened," and "Two men wrestled," don't seem to me at all the same; but I dare say I read old books of logic. Well, it's like that here. You seem to be all certain this man is a murderer. But I never said he was a murderer. I said he was the man we wanted. He is. I want him very much. I want him frightfully. I want him as the one thing we haven't got in the whole of this horrible case – a witness!'

They all stared at him, but in a frowning fashion, like men trying to follow a sharp new turn of the argument; and it was he who resumed the argument.

'From the first minute I entered that big empty bar or saloon, I knew what was the matter with all this business was emptiness; solitude; too many chances for anybody to be alone. In a word, the absence of witnesses. All we knew was that when we came in, the manager and the barman were not in the bar. But when *were* they in the bar? What chance was there of making any sort of time-table of when anybody was anywhere? The whole thing was blank for want of witnesses. I rather fancy the barman or somebody was in the bar just before we came; and that's how the Scotchman got his Scotch whisky. He certainly didn't get it after we came. But we can't begin to inquire whether anybody in the hotel poisoned poor Raggley's cherry brandy, till we really know who was in the bar and when. Now I want you to do me another favour, in spite of this stupid muddle, which is probably all my fault. I want you to collect all the people involved in this room – I think they're all still available, unless the Asiatic has gone back to Asia – and then take the poor Scotchman out of his handcuffs, and bring him in here, and let him tell us who did serve him with whisky, and who was in the bar, and who else was in the room, and all the rest. He's the only man whose evidence can cover just that period when the crime was done. I don't see the slightest reason for doubting his word.'

'But look here,' said Greenwood. 'This brings it all back to the hotel authorities; and I thought you agreed that the manager isn't the murderer. Is it the barman, or what?'

'I don't know,' said the priest blankly. 'I don't know for certain even about the manager. I don't know anything about the barman. I fancy the manager might be a bit of a conspirator, even if he wasn't a murderer. But I do know there's one solitary witness on earth who may have seen something; and that's why I set all your police dogs on his trail to the ends of the earth.'

The mysterious Scotchman, when he finally appeared before the company thus assembled, was certainly a formidable figure; tall, with a hulking stride and a long sardonic hatchet face, with tufts of red hair; and wearing not only an Inverness cape but a Glengarry bonnet. He might well be excused for a somewhat acrid attitude; but anybody could see he was of the sort to resist arrest, even with violence. It was not surprising that he had come to blows with a fighting fellow like Raggley. It was not even surprising that the police had been convinced, by the mere details of capture, that he was a tough and a typical killer. But he claimed to be a perfectly respectable farmer, in Aberdeen-shire, his name being James Grant; and somehow not only Father Brown, but Inspector Greenwood, a shrewd man with a great deal of experience, was pretty soon convinced that the Scot's ferocity was the fury of innocence rather than guilt.

'Now what we want from you, Mr Grant,' said the Inspector gravely, dropping without further parley into tones of courtesy, 'is simply your evidence on one very important fact. I am greatly grieved at the misunderstanding by which you have suffered, but I am sure you wish to serve the ends of justice. I believe you came into this bar just after it opened, at half-past five, and were served with a glass of whisky. We are not certain what servant of the hotel, whether the barman or the manager or some subordinate, was in the bar at that time. Will you look round the room, and tell me whether the bar-attendant who served you is present here.'

'Aye, he's present,' said Mr Grant, grimly smiling, having swept the group with a shrewd glance. 'I'd know him anywhere; and ye'll agree he's big enough to be seen. Do ye have all your inn-servants as grand as yon?'

The Inspector's eye remained hard and steady, and his voice colourless and continuous; the face of Father Brown was a blank; but on many other faces there was a cloud; the barman was not particularly big and not at all grand; and the manager was decidedly small.

'We only want the barman identified,' said the Inspector calmly. 'Of course we know him; but we should like you to verify it independently. You mean ...?' And he stopped suddenly.

'Weel, there he is plain enough, 'said the Scotchman wearily; and made a gesture, and with that gesture the gigantic Jukes, the prince of commercial travellers, rose like a trumpeting elephant; and in a flash had three policemen fastened on him like hounds on a wild beast.

'Well, all that was simple enough,' said Father Brown to his friend afterwards. 'As I told you, the instant I entered the empty bar-room, my first thought was that, if the barman left the bar unguarded like that, there was nothing in the world to stop you or me or anybody else lifting the flap and walking in, and putting poison in any of the bottles standing waiting for customers. Of course, a practical poisoner would probably do it as Jukes did, by substituting a poisoned bottle for the ordinary bottle; that could be done in a flash. It was easy enough for him, as he travelled in bottles, to carry a flask of cherry brandy prepared and of the same pattern. Of course, it requires one condition; but it's a fairly common condition. It would hardly do to start poisoning the beer or whisky that scores of people drink; it would cause a massacre. But when a man is well known as drinking only one special thing, like cherry brandy, that isn't very widely drunk, it's just like poisoning him in his own home. Only it's a jolly sight safer. For practically the whole suspicion instantly falls on the hotel, or somebody to do with the hotel; and there's no earthly argument to show that it was done by anyone out of a hundred customers that might come into the bar: even if people realized that a customer could do it. It was about as absolutely anonymous and irresponsible a murder as a man could commit.'

'And why exactly did the murderer commit it?' asked his friend.

Father Brown rose and gravely gathered the papers which he had previously scattered in a moment of distraction.

'May I recall your attention,' he said smiling, 'to the materials of the forthcoming Life and Letters of the Late John Raggley? Or, for that matter, his own spoken words? He said in this very bar that he was going to expose a scandal about the management of hotels; and the scandal was the pretty common one of a corrupt agreement between hotel proprietors and a salesman who took and gave secret commissions, so that his business had a monopoly of all the drink sold in the place. It wasn't even an open slavery like an ordinary tied house; it was a swindle at the expense of everybody the manager was supposed to serve. It was a legal offence. So the ingenious Jukes, taking the first moment when the bar was empty, as it often was, stepped inside and made the exchange of bottles; unfortunately at that very moment a Scotchman in an Inverness cape came in harshly demanding whisky. Jukes saw his only chance was to pretend to be the barman and serve the customer. He was very much relieved that the customer was a Quick One.'

'I think you're rather a Quick One yourself,' observed Greenwood; 'if you say you smelt something at the start, in the mere air of an empty room. Did you suspect Jukes at all at the start?'

'Well, he sounded rather rich somehow,' answered Father Brown vaguely. 'You know when a man has a rich voice. And I did sort of ask myself why he should have such a disgustingly rich voice, when all those honest fellows were fairly poor. But I think I knew he was a sham when I saw that big shining breast-pin.'

'You mean because it was sham?' asked Greenwood doubt-fully.

'Oh, no; because it was genuine,' said Father Brown.

THREE

The Blast of the Book

PROFESSOR OPENSHAW always lost his temper, with a loud
bang, if anybody called him a Spiritualist; or a believer in
Spiritualism. This, however, did not exhaust his explosive
elements; for he also lost his temper if anybody called him a
disbeliever in Spiritualism. It was his pride to have given his
whole life to investigating Psychic Phenomena; it was also his
pride never to have given a hint of whether he thought they were
really psychic or merely phenomenal. He enjoyed nothing so
much as to sit in a circle of devout Spiritualists and give devas-
tating descriptions of how he had exposed medium after medium
and detected fraud after fraud; for indeed he was a man of much
detective talent and insight, when once he had fixed his eye on an
object, and he always fixed his eye on a medium, as a highly
suspicious object. There was a story of his having spotted the
same Spiritualist mountebank under three different disguises:
dressed as a woman, a white-bearded old man, and a Brahmin
of a rich chocolate brown. These recitals made the true believers
rather restless, as indeed they were intended to do; but they
could hardly complain, for no Spiritualist denies the existence of fraudulent mediums; only the Professor's flowing
narrative might well seem to indicate that all mediums were
fraudulent.

But woe to the simple-minded and innocent Materialist (and
Materialists as a race are rather innocent and simple-minded)
who, presuming on this narrative tendency, should advance
the thesis that ghosts were against the laws of nature, or that
such things were only old superstitions; or that it was all tosh,
or, alternatively, bunk. Him would the Professor, suddenly
reversing all his scientific batteries, sweep from the field with a
cannonade of unquestionable cases and unexplained phenomena,

47

of which the wretched rationalist had never heard in his life, giving all the dates and details, stating all the attempted and abandoned natural explanations; stating everything, indeed, except whether he, John Oliver Openshaw, did or did not believe in Spirits; and that neither Spiritualist nor Materialist could ever boast of finding out.

Professor Openshaw, a lean figure with pale leonine hair and hypnotic blue eyes, stood exchanging a few words with Father Brown, who was a friend of his, on the steps outside the hotel where both had been breakfasting that morning and sleeping the night before. The Professor had come back rather late from one of his grand experiments, in general exasperation, and was still tingling with the fight that he always waged alone and against both sides.

'Oh, I don't mind you,' he said laughing. 'You don't believe in it even if it's true. But all these people are perpetually asking me what I'm trying to prove. They don't seem to understand that I'm a man of science. A man of science isn't trying to prove anything. He's trying to find out what will prove itself.'

'But he hasn't found out yet,' said Father Brown.

'Well, I have some little notions of my own, that are not quite so negative as most people think,' answered the Professor, after an instant of frowning silence; 'anyhow, I've begun to fancy that if there is something to be found, they're looking for it along the wrong line. It's all too theatrical; it's showing off, all their shiny ectoplasm and trumpets and voices and the rest; all on the model of old melodramas and mouldy historical novels about the Family Ghost. If they'd go to history instead of historical novels, I'm beginning to think they'd really find something. But not Apparitions.'

'After all,' said Father Brown, 'Apparitions are only Appearances. I suppose you'd say the Family Ghost is only keeping up appearances.'

The Professor's gaze, which had commonly a fine abstracted character, suddenly fixed and focused itself as it did on a dubious medium. It had rather the air of a man screwing a strong magnifying-glass into his eye. Not that he thought the priest was in the least like a dubious medium; but he was startled

48

into attention by his friend's thought following so closely on his own.

'Appearances!' he muttered, 'crikey, but it's odd you should say that just now. The more I learn, the more I fancy they lose by merely looking for appearances. Now if they'd look a little into Disappearances –'

'Yes,' said Father Brown, 'after all, the real fairy legends weren't so very much about the appearance of famous fairies; calling up Titania or exhibiting Oberon by moonlight. But there were no end of legends about people *disappearing*, because they were stolen by the fairies. Are you on the track of Kilmeny or Thomas the Rhymer?'

'I'm on the track of ordinary modern people you've read of in the newspapers,' answered Openshaw. 'You may well stare; but that's my game just now; and I've been on it for a long time. Frankly, I think a lot of psychic appearances could be explained away. It's the disappearances I can't explain, unless they're psychic. These people in the newspapers who vanish and are never found – if you knew the details as I do ... and now only this morning I got confirmation; an extraordinary letter from an old missionary, quite a respectable old boy. He's coming to see me at my office this morning. Perhaps you'd lunch with me or something; and I'd tell the results – in confidence.'

'Thanks; I will – unless,' said Father Brown modestly, 'the fairies have stolen me by then.'

With that they parted and Openshaw walked round the corner to a small office he rented in the neighbourhood; chiefly for the publication of a small periodical, of psychical and psychological notes of the driest and most agnostic sort. He had only one clerk, who sat at a desk in the outer office, totting up figures and facts for the purposes of the printed report; and the Professor paused to ask if Mr Pringle had called. The clerk answered mechanically in the negative and went on mechanically adding up figures; and the Professor turned towards the inner room that was his study. 'Oh, by the way, Berridge,' he added, without turning round, 'if Mr Pringle comes, send him straight in to me. You needn't interrupt your work; I rather want those notes finished tonight if possible. You might leave them on my desk tomorrow, if I am late.'

And he went into his private office, still brooding on the problem which the name of Pringle had raised; or rather, perhaps, had ratified and confirmed in his mind. Even the most perfectly balanced of agnostics is partially human; and it is possible that the missionary's letter seemed to have greater weight as promising to support his private and still tentative hypothesis. He sat down in his large and comfortable chair, opposite the engraving of Montaigne; and read once more the short letter from the Rev. Luke Pringle, making the appointment for that morning. No man knew better than Professor Openshaw the marks of the letter of the crank; the crowded details; the spidery handwriting; the unnecessary length and repetition. There were none of these things in this case; but a brief and businesslike typewritten statement that the writer had encountered some curious cases of Disappearance, which seemed to fall within the province of the Professor as a student of psychic problems. The Professor was favourably impressed; nor had he any unfavourable impression, in spite of a slight movement of surprise, when he looked up and saw that the Rev. Luke Pringle was already in the room.

'Your clerk told me I was to come straight in,' said Mr Pringle apologetically, but with a broad and rather agreeable grin. The grin was partly masked by masses of reddish-grey beard and whiskers; a perfect jungle of a beard, such as is sometimes grown by white men living in the jungles; but the eyes above the snub nose had nothing about them in the least wild or outlandish. Openshaw had instantly turned on them that concentrated spotlight or burning-glass of sceptical scrutiny which he turned on many men to see if they were mountebanks or maniacs; and, in this case, he had a rather unusual sense of reassurance. The wild beard might have belonged to a crank, but the eyes completely contradicted the beard; they were full of that quite frank and friendly laughter which is never found in the faces of those who are serious frauds or serious lunatics. He would have expected a man with those eyes to be a Philistine, a jolly sceptic, a man who shouted out shallow but hearty contempt of ghosts and spirits; but anyhow, no professional humbug could afford to look as frivolous as that. The man was buttoned up to the throat in a shabby old cape, and only his broad limp hat suggested the cleric; but missionaries from wild places do not always bother to dress like clerics.

'You probably think all this is another hoax, Professor,' said Mr Pringle, with a sort of abstract enjoyment, 'and I hope you will forgive my laughing at your very natural air of disapproval. All the same, I've got to tell my story to somebody who knows, because it's true. And, all joking apart, it's tragic as well as true. Well, to cut it short, I was missionary in Nya-Nya, a station in West Africa, in the thick of the forests, where almost the only other white man was the officer in command of the district, Captain Wales; and he and I grew rather thick. Not that he liked missions; he was, if I may say so, thick in many ways; one of those square-headed, square-shouldered men of action who hardly need to think, let alone believe. That's what makes it all the queerer. One day he came back to his tent in the forest, after a short leave, and said he had gone through a jolly rum experience, and didn't know what to do about it. He was holding a rusty old book in a leather binding, and he put it down on a table beside his revolver and an old Arab sword he kept, probably as a curiosity. He said this book had belonged to a man on the boat he had just come off; and the man swore that nobody must open the book, or look inside it; or else they would be carried off by the devil, or disappear, or something. Wales said this was all nonsense, of course; and they had a quarrel; and the upshot seems to have been that this man, taunted with cowardice or superstition, actually did look into the book; and instantly dropped it; walked to the side of the boat – '

'One moment,' said the Professor, who had made one or two notes. 'Before you tell me anything else. Did this man tell Wales where he had got the book, or who it originally belonged to?'

'Yes, replied Pringle, now entirely grave. 'It seems he said he was bringing it back to Dr Hankey, the Oriental traveller now in England, to whom it originally belonged, and who had warned him of its strange properties. Well, Hankey is an able man and a

51

rather crabbed and sneering sort of man; which makes it queerer still. But the point of Wales's story is much simpler. It is that the man who had looked into the book walked straight over the side of the ship, and was never seen again.'

'Do you believe it yourself?' asked Openshaw after a pause.

'Well, I do,' replied Pringle. 'I believe it for two reasons. First, that Wales was an entirely unimaginative man; and he added one touch that only an imaginative man could have added. He said that the man walked straight over the side on a still and calm day; but there was no splash.'

The Professor looked at his notes for some seconds in silence; and then said: 'And your other reason for believing it?'

'My other reason,' answered the Rev. Luke Pringle, 'is what I saw myself.'

There was another silence; until he continued in the same matter-of-fact way. Whatever he had, he had nothing of the eagerness with which the crank, or even the believer, tried to convince others.

'I told you that Wales put down the book on the table beside the sword. There was only one entrance to the tent; and it happened that I was standing in it, looking out into the forest, with my back to my companion. He was standing by the table grumbling and growling about the whole business; saying it was tomfoolery in the twentieth century to be frightened of opening a book; asking why the devil he shouldn't open it himself. Then some instinct stirred in me and I said he had better not do that, it had better be returned to Dr Hankey. "What harm could it do?" he said restlessly. "What harm did it do?" I answered obstinately. "What happened to your friend on the boat?" He didn't answer, indeed I didn't know what he could answer; but I pressed my logical advantage in mere vanity. "If it comes to that," I said, "what is your version of what really happened on the boat?" Still he didn't answer; and I looked round and saw that he wasn't there.

'The tent was empty. The book was lying on the table; open, but on its face, as if he had turned it downwards. But the sword was lying on the ground near the other side of the tent; and the canvas of the tent showed a great slash, as if somebody had hacked his way out with the sword. The gash in the tent gaped at me; but showed only the dark glimmer of the forest outside. And when I went across and looked through the rent I could not be certain whether the tangle of the tall plants and the undergrowth had been bent or broken; at least not farther than a few feet. I have never seen or heard of Captain Wales from that day.

'I wrapped the book up in brown paper, taking good care not to look at it; and I brought it back to England, intending at first to return it to Dr Hankey. Then I saw some notes in your paper suggesting a hypothesis about such things; and I decided to stop on the way and put the matter before you; as you have a name for being balanced and having an open mind.'

Professor Openshaw laid down his pen and looked steadily at the man on the other side of the table; concentrating in that single stare all his long experience of many entirely different types of humbug, and even some eccentric and extraordinary types of honest men. In the ordinary way, he would have begun with the healthy hypothesis that the story was a pack of lies. On the whole he did incline to assume that it was a pack of lies. And yet he could not fit the man into his story; if it were only that he could not see that sort of liar telling that sort of lie. The man was not trying to look honest on the surface, as most quacks and impostors do; somehow, it seemed all the other way; as if the man *was* honest, in spite of something else that was merely on the surface. He thought of a good man with one innocent delusion; but again the symptoms were not the same; there was even a sort of virile indifference; as if the man did not care much about his delusion, if it was a delusion.

'Mr Pringle,' he said sharply, like a barrister making a witness jump, 'where is this book of yours now?'

The grin reappeared on the bearded face which had grown grave during the recital.

'I left it outside,' said Mr Pringle. 'I mean in the outer office. It was a risk, perhaps; but the less risk of the two.'

'What do you mean?' demanded the Professor. 'Why didn't you bring it straight in here?'

'Because,' answered the missionary, 'I knew that as soon as

you saw it, you'd open it – before you had heard the story.
I thought it possible you might think twice about opening it –
after you'd heard the story.'

Then after a silence he added: 'There was nobody out there
but your clerk; and he looked a stolid steady-going specimen,
immersed in business calculations.'

Openshaw laughed unaffectedly. 'Oh, Babbage,' he cried, 'your
magic tomes are safe enough with him, I assure you. His name's
Berridge – but I often call him Babbage; because he's so exactly
like a Calculating Machine. No human being, if you can call him
a human being, would be less likely to open other people's
brown paper parcels. Well, we may as well go and bring it in
now; though I assure you I will consider seriously the course
to be taken with it. Indeed, I tell you frankly,' and he stared at the
man again, 'that I'm not quite sure whether we ought to open
it here and now, or send it to this Dr Hankey.'

The two had passed together out of the inner into the outer
office; and even as they did so, Mr Pringle gave a cry and ran
forward towards the clerk's desk. For the clerk's desk was there;
but not the clerk. On the clerk's desk lay a faded old leather
book, torn out of its brown-paper wrappings, and lying closed,
but as if it had just been opened. The clerk's desk stood against
the wide window that looked out into the street; and the window
was shattered with a huge ragged hole in the glass; as if a human
body had been shot through it into the world without. There
was no other trace of Mr Berridge.

Both the two men left in the office stood as still as statues; and
then it was the Professor who slowly came to life. He looked even
more judicial than he had ever looked in his life, as he slowly
turned and held out his hand to the missionary.

'Mr Pringle,' he said, 'I beg your pardon. I beg your pardon
only for thoughts that I have had; and half-thoughts at that.
But nobody could call himself a scientific man and not face a
fact like this.'

'I suppose,' said Pringle doubtfully, 'that we ought to make
some inquiries. Can you ring up his house and find out if he has
gone home?'

'I don't know that he's on the telephone,' answered Openshaw, rather absently; 'he lives somewhere up Hampstead way, I think. But I suppose somebody will inquire here, if his friends or family miss him.'

'Could we furnish a description,' asked the other, 'if the police want it?'

'The police!' said the Professor, starting from his reverie. 'A description ... Well, he looked awfully like everybody else, I'm afraid, except for goggles. One of those clean-shaven chaps. But the police ... look here, what *are* we to do about this mad business?'

'I know what I ought to do,' said the Rev. Mr Pringle firmly, 'I am going to take this book straight to the only original Dr Hankey, and ask him what the devil it's all about. He lives not very far from here, and I'll come straight back and tell you what he says.'

'Oh, very well,' said the Professor at last, as he sat down rather wearily; perhaps relieved for the moment to be rid of the responsibility. But long after the brisk and ringing footsteps of the little missionary had died away down the street, the Professor sat in the same posture, staring into vacancy like a man in a trance.

He was still in the same seat and almost in the same attitude, when the same brisk footsteps were heard on the pavement without and the missionary entered, this time, as a glance assured him, with empty hands.

'Dr Hankey,' said Pringle gravely, 'wants to keep the book for an hour and consider the point. Then he asks us both to call, and he will give us his decision. He specially desired, Professor, that you should accompany me on the second visit.'

Openshaw continued to stare in silence; then he said, suddenly:

'Who the devil is Dr Hankey?'

'You sound rather as if you meant he was the devil,' said Pringle, smiling, 'and I fancy some people have thought so. He had quite a reputation in your own line; but he gained it mostly in India, studying local magic and so on, so perhaps he's not so well known here. He is a yellow skinny little devil with a lame leg, and a doubtful temper; but he seems to have set up in an ordinary respectable practice in these parts, and I don't know anything definitely wrong about him – unless it's wrong to be the only person who can possibly know anything about all this crazy affair.'

Professor Openshaw rose heavily and went to the telephone; he rang up Father Brown, changing the luncheon engagement to a dinner, that he might hold himself free for the expedition to the house of the Anglo-Indian doctor; after that he sat down again, lit a cigar and sank once more into his own unfathomable thoughts.

Father Brown went round to the restaurant appointed for dinner, and kicked his heels for some time in a vestibule full of mirrors and palms in pots; he had been informed of Openshaw's afternoon engagement, and, as the evening closed-in dark and stormy round the glass and the green plants, guessed that it had produced something unexpected and unduly prolonged. He even wondered for a moment whether the Professor would turn up at all; but when the Professor eventually did, it was clear that his own more general guesses had been justified. For it was a very wild-eyed and even wild-haired Professor who eventually drove back with Mr Pringle from the expedition to the North of London, where suburbs are still fringed with heathy wastes and scraps of common, looking more sombre under the rather thunderstorm sunset. Nevertheless, they had apparently found the house, standing a little apart though within hail of other houses; they had verified the brass-plate duly engraved: 'J. I. Hankey, MD, MRCS.' Only they did not find J. I. Hankey, MD, MRCS. They found only what a nightmare whisper had already subconsciously prepared them to find: a commonplace parlour with the accursed volume lying on the table, as if it had just been read; and beyond, a back door burst open and a faint trail of footsteps that ran a little way up so steep a garden-path that it seemed that no lame man could have run up so lightly. But it was a lame man who had run; for in those few steps there was the misshapen unequal mark of some sort of surgical boot; then two marks of that boot alone (as if the creature had hopped) and then nothing. There was nothing further to be learnt from

Dr J. I. Hankey, except that he had made his decision. He had read the oracle and received the doom.

When the two came into the entrance under the palms, Pringle put the book down suddenly on a small table, as if it burned his fingers. The priest glanced at it curiously; there was only some rude lettering on the front with a couplet:

> They that looked into this book
> Them the Flying Terror took;

and underneath, as he afterwards discovered, similar warnings in Greek, Latin and French. The other two had turned away with a natural impulsion towards drinks, after their exhaustion and bewilderment; and Openshaw had called to the waiter, who brought cocktails on a tray.

'You will dine with us, I hope,' said the Professor to the missionary; but Mr Pringle amiably shook his head.

'If you'll forgive me,' he said, 'I'm going off to wrestle with this book and this business by myself somewhere. I suppose I couldn't use your office for an hour or so?'

'I suppose – I'm afraid it's locked,' said Openshaw in some surprise.

'You forget there's a hole in the window.' The Rev. Luke Pringle gave the very broadest of all his broad grins and vanished into the darkness without.

'A rather odd fellow, that, after all,' said the Professor, frowning.

He was rather surprised to find Father Brown talking to the waiter who had brought the cocktails, apparently about the waiter's most private affairs; for there was some mention of a baby who was now out of danger. He commented on the fact with some surprise, wondering how the priest came to know the man; but the former only said, 'Oh, I dine here every two or three months, and I've talked to him now and then.'

The Professor, who himself dined there about five times a week, was conscious that he had never thought of talking to the man; but his thoughts were interrupted by a strident ringing and a summons to the telephone. The voice on the telephone said it was Pringle; it was rather a muffled voice, but it might well be muffled in all those bushes of beard and whisker. Its message was enough to establish identity.

'Professor,' said the voice, 'I can't stand it any longer. I'm going to look for myself. I'm speaking from your office and the book is in front of me. If anything happens to me, this is to say good-bye. No – it's no good trying to stop me. You wouldn't be in time anyhow. I'm opening the book now. I . . .'

Openshaw thought he heard something like a sort of thrilling or shivering yet almost soundless crash; then he shouted the name of Pringle again and again; but he heard no more. He hung up the receiver, and, restored to a superb academic calm, rather like the calm of despair, went back and quietly took his seat at the dinner-table. Then, as coolly as if he were describing the failure of some small silly trick at a séance, he told the priest every detail of this monstrous mystery.

'Five men have now vanished in thi impossible way,' he said. 'Every one is extraordinary; and yet the one case I simply can't get over is my clerk, Berridge. It's just because he was the quietest creature that he's the queerest case.'

'Yes,' replied Father Brown, 'it was a queer thing for Berridge to do, anyway. He was awfully conscientious. He was also so jolly careful to keep all the office business separate from any fun of his own. Why, hardly anybody knew he was quite a humorist at home and –'

'Berridge!' cried the Professor. 'What on earth are you talking about? Did you know him?'

'Oh no,' said Father Brown carelessly, 'only as you say I know the waiter. I've often had to wait in your office, till you turned up; and of course I passed the time of day with poor Berridge. He was rather a card. I remember he once said he would like to collect valueless things, as collectors did the silly things they thought valuable. You know the old story about the woman who collected valueless things.'

'I'm not sure I know what you're talking about,' said Openshaw. 'But even if my clerk was eccentric (and I never knew a man I should have thought less so), it wouldn't explain what happened to him; and it certainly wouldn't explain the others.'

'What others?' asked the priest.

The Professor stared at him and spoke distinctly, as if to a child:

'My dear Father Brown, Five Men have disappeared.'

'My dear Professor Openshaw, no men have disappeared.'

Father Brown gazed back at his host with equal steadiness and spoke with equal distinctness. Nevertheless, the Professor required the words repeated, and they were repeated as distinctly.

'I say that no men have disappeared.'

After a moment's silence, he added, 'I suppose the hardest thing is to convince anybody that $0 + 0 + 0 = 0$. Men believe the oddest things if they are in a series; that is why Macbeth believed the three words of the three witches; though the first was something he knew himself; and the last something he could only bring about himself. But in your case the middle term is the weakest of all.'

'What do you mean?'

'You saw nobody vanish. You did not see the man vanish from the boat. You did not see the man vanish from the tent. All that rests on the word of Mr Pringle, which I will not discuss just now. But you'll admit this; you would never have taken his word yourself, *unless* you had seen it confirmed by your clerk's disappearance; just as Macbeth would never have believed he would be king, if he had not been confirmed in believing he would be Cawdor.'

'That may be true,' said the Professor, nodding slowly. 'But *when* it was confirmed, I knew it was the truth. You say I saw nothing myself. But I did; I saw my own clerk disappear. Berridge did disappear.'

'Berridge did not disappear,' said Father Brown. 'On the contrary.'

'What the devil do you mean by "on the contrary"?'

'I mean,' said Father Brown, 'that he never disappeared. He appeared.'

Openshaw stared across at his friend, but the eyes had already altered in his head, as they did when they concentrated on a new presentation of a problem. The priest went on:

'He appeared in your study, disguised in a bushy red beard and buttoned up in a clumsy cape, and announced himself as the Rev. Luke Pringle. And you had never noticed your own clerk enough to know him again, when he was in so rough-and-ready a disguise.'

'But surely,' began the Professor.

'Could you describe him for the police?' asked Father Brown. 'Not you. You probably knew he was clean-shaven and wore tinted glasses; and merely taking off those glasses was a better disguise than putting on anything else. You had never seen his eyes any more than his soul; jolly laughing eyes. He had planted his absurd book and all the properties; then he calmly smashed the window, put on the beard and cape and walked into your study; knowing that you had never looked at him in your life.'

'But why should he play me such an insane trick?' demanded Openshaw.

'Why, *because* you had never looked at him in your life,' said Father Brown; and his hand slightly curled and clinched, as if he might have struck the table, if he had been given to gesture. 'You called him the Calculating Machine, because that was all you ever used him for. You never found out even what a stranger strolling into your office could find out, in five minutes' chat: that he was a character; that he was full of antics; that he had all sorts of views on you and your theories and your reputation for "spotting" people. Can't you understand his itching to prove that you couldn't spot your own clerk? He has nonsense notions of all sorts. About collecting useless things, for instance. Don't you know the story of the woman who bought the two most useless things: an old doctor's brass-plate and a wooden leg? With those your ingenious clerk created the character of the remarkable Dr Hankey; as easily as the visionary Captain Wales. Planting them in his own house –'

'Do you mean that place we visited beyond Hampstead was Berridge's own house?' asked Openshaw.

'Did *you* know his house – or even his address?' retorted the priest. 'Look here, don't think I'm speaking disrespectfully of you or your work. You are a great servant of truth and you know I could never be disrespectful to that. You've seen through a lot of liars, when you put your mind to it. But don't *only* look at liars. Do, just occasionally, look at honest men – like the waiter.'

'Where is Berridge now?' asked the Professor, after a long silence.

'I haven't the least doubt,' said Father Brown, 'that he is back in your office. In fact, he came back into your office at the exact moment when the Rev. Luke Pringle read the awful volume and faded into the void.'

There was another long silence and then Professor Openshaw laughed; with the laugh of a great man who is great enough to look small. Then he said abruptly:

'I suppose I do deserve it; for not noticing the nearest helpers I have. But you must admit the accumulation of incidents was rather formidable. Did you *never* feel just a momentary awe of the awful volume?'

'Oh, that,' said Father Brown. 'I opened it as soon as I saw it lying there. It's all blank pages. You see, I am not superstitious.'

FOUR

The Green Man

A YOUNG man in knickerbockers, with an eager sanguine profile, was playing golf against himself on the links that lay parallel to the sand and sea, which were all growing grey with twilight. He was not carelessly knocking a ball about, but rather practising particular strokes with a sort of microscopic fury; like a neat and tidy whirlwind. He had learned many games quickly, but he had a disposition to learn them a little more quickly than they can be learnt. He was rather prone to be a victim of those remarkable invitations by which a man may learn the Violin in Six Lessons – or acquire a perfect French accent by a Correspondence Course. He lived in the breezy atmosphere of such hopeful advertisement and adventure. He was at present the private secretary of Admiral Sir Michael Craven, who owned the big house behind the park abutting on the links. He was ambitious, and had no intention of continuing indefinitely to be private secretary to anybody. But he was also reasonable; and he knew that the best way of ceasing to be a secretary was to be a good secretary. Consequently he was a very good secretary; dealing with the ever-accumulating arrears of the Admiral's correspondence with the same swift centripetal concentration with which he addressed the golf-ball. He had to struggle with the correspondence alone and at his own discretion at present; for the Admiral had been with his ship for the last six months; and, though now returning, was not expected for hours, or possibly days.

With an athletic stride, the young man, whose name was Harold Harker, crested the rise of turf that was the rampart of the links and, looking out across the sands to the sea, saw a strange sight. He did not see it very clearly; for the dusk was darkening every minute under stormy clouds; but it seemed to him, by a sort of momentary illusion, like a dream of days long past or a drama played by ghosts, out of another age in history.

The last of the sunset lay in long bars of copper and gold above the last dark strip of sea that seemed rather black than blue. But blacker still against this gleam in the west, there passed in sharp outline, like figures in a shadow pantomime, two men with three-cornered cocked hats and swords; as if they had just landed from one of the wooden ships of Nelson. It was not at all the sort of hallucination that would have come natural to Mr Harker, had he been prone to hallucinations. He was of the type that is at once sanguine and scientific; and would be more likely to fancy the flying-ships of the future than the fighting-ships of the past. He therefore very sensibly came to the conclusion that even a futurist can believe his eyes.

His illusion did not last more than a moment. On the second glance, what he saw was unusual but not incredible. The two men who were striding in single file across the sands, one some fifteen yards behind the other, were ordinary modern naval officers; but naval officers wearing that almost extravagant full-dress uniform which naval officers never do wear if they can possibly help it; only on great ceremonial occasions such as the visits of Royalty. In the man walking in front, who seemed more or less unconscious of the man walking behind, Harker recognized at once the high-bridged nose and spike-shaped beard of his own employer the Admiral. The other man following in his tracks he did not know. But he did know something about the circumstances connected with the ceremonial occasion. He knew that when the Admiral's ship put in at the adjacent port, it was to be formally visited by a Great Personage; which was enough, in that sense, to explain the officers being in full dress. But he did also know the officers; or at any rate the Admiral. And what could have possessed the Admiral to come on shore in that rig-out, when one could swear he would seize five minutes to change into mufti or at least into undress uniform, was more than his secretary could conceive. It seemed somehow to be the very last thing he would do. It was indeed to remain for many weeks one of the chief mysteries of this mysterious business. As it was, the outline of these fantastic court uniforms against the empty scenery, striped with dark sea and sand, had something suggestive of comic opera; and reminded the spectator of *Pinafore*.

The second figure was much more singular; somewhat singular in appearance, despite his correct lieutenant's uniform, and still more extraordinary in behaviour. He walked in a strangely irregular and uneasy manner; sometimes quickly and sometimes slowly; as if he could not make up his mind whether to overtake the Admiral or not. The Admiral was rather deaf and certainly heard no footsteps behind him on the yielding sand; but the footsteps behind him, if traced in the detective manner, would have given rise to twenty conjectures from a limp to a dance. The man's face was swarthy as well as darkened with shadow and every now and then the eyes in it shifted and shone, as if to accent his agitation. Once he began to run and then abruptly relapsed into a swaggering slowness and carelessness. Then he did something which Mr Harker could never have conceived any normal naval officer in His Britannic Majesty's Service doing, even in a lunatic asylum. He drew his sword.

It was at this bursting-point of the prodigy that the two passing figures disappeared behind a headland on the shore. The staring secretary had just time to notice the swarthy stranger, with a resumption of carelessness, knock off a head of sea-holly with his glittering blade. He seemed then to have abandoned all idea of catching the other man up. But Mr Harold Harker's face became very thoughtful indeed; and he stood there ruminating for some time before he gravely took himself inland, towards the road that ran past the gates of the great house and so by a long curve down to the sea.

It was up this curving road from the coast that the Admiral might be expected to come, considering the direction in which he had been walking, and making the natural assumption that he was bound for his own door. The path along the sands, under the links, turned inland just beyond the headland and solidifying itself into a road, returned towards Craven House. It was down this road, therefore, that the secretary darted, with characteristic impetuosity, to meet his patron returning home. But the patron was apparently not returning home. What was still more peculiar, the secretary was not returning home either;

at least until many hours later; a delay quite long enough to arouse alarm and mystification at Craven House.

Behind the pillars and palms of that rather too palatial country house, indeed, there was expectancy gradually changing to uneasiness. Gryce the butler, a big bilious man abnormally silent below as well as above stairs, showed a certain restlessness as he moved about the main front-hall and occasionally looked out of the side windows of the porch, on the white road that swept towards the sea. The Admiral's sister Marion, who kept house for him, had her brother's high nose with a more sniffy expression; she was voluble, rather rambling, not without humour, and capable of sudden emphasis as shrill as a cockatoo. The Admiral's daughter Olive was dark, dreamy, and as a rule abstractedly silent, perhaps melancholy; so that her aunt generally conducted most of the conversation, and that without reluctance. But the girl also had a gift of sudden laughter that was very engaging.

'I can't think why they're not here already,' said the elder lady. 'The postman distinctly told me he'd seen the Admiral coming along the beach; along with that dreadful creature Rook. Why in the world they call him Lieutenant Rook –'

'Perhaps,' suggested the melancholy young lady, with a momentary brightness, 'perhaps they call him Lieutenant because he is a Lieutenant.'

'I can't think why the Admiral keeps him,' snorted her aunt, as if she were talking of a housemaid. She was very proud of her brother and always called him the Admiral; but her notions of a commission in the Senior Service were inexact.

'Well, Roger Rook is sulky and unsociable and all that,' replied Olive, 'but of course that wouldn't prevent him being a capable sailor.'

'Sailor!' cried her aunt with one of her rather startling cockatoo notes, 'he isn't my notion of a sailor. The Lass that Loved a Sailor, as they used to sing when I was young . . . Just think of it! He's not gay and free and whatsitsname. He doesn't sing chanties or dance a hornpipe.'

'Well,' observed her niece with gravity. 'The Admiral doesn't very often dance a hornpipe.'

'Oh, you know what I mean – he isn't bright or breezy or anything,' replied the old lady. 'Why, that secretary fellow could do better than that.'

Olive's rather tragic face was transfigured by one of her good and rejuvenating waves of laughter.

'I'm sure Mr Harker would dance a hornpipe for you,' she said, 'and say he had learnt it in half an hour from the book of instructions. He's always learning things of that sort.'

She stopped laughing suddenly and looked at her aunt's rather strained face.

'I can't think why Mr Harker doesn't come,' she added.

'I don't care about Mr Harker,' replied the aunt, and rose and looked out of the window.

The evening light had long turned from yellow to grey and was now turning almost to white under the widening moonlight, over the large flat landscape by the coast; unbroken by any features save a clump of sea-twisted trees round a pool and beyond, rather gaunt and dark against the horizon, the shabby fishermen's tavern on the shore that bore the name of the Green Man. And all that road and landscape was empty of any living thing. Nobody had seen the figure in the cocked hat that had been observed, earlier in the evening, walking by the sea; or the other and stranger figure that had been seen trailing after him. Nobody had even seen the secretary who saw them.

It was after midnight when the secretary at last burst in and aroused the household; and his face, white as a ghost, looked all the paler against the background of the stolid face and figure of a big Inspector of Police. Somehow that red, heavy, indifferent face looked, even more than the white and harassed one, like a mask of doom. The news was broken to the two women with such consideration or concealments as were possible. But the news was that the body of Admiral Craven had been eventually fished out of the foul weeds and scum of the pool under the trees; and that he was drowned and dead.

Anybody acquainted with Mr Harold Harker, secretary, will realize that, whatever his agitation, he was by morning in a mood to be tremendously on the spot. He hustled the Inspector, whom he had met the night before on the road down by the Green Man, into another room for private and practical consultation. He questioned the Inspector rather as the Inspector might have questioned a yokel. But Inspector Burns was a stolid character; and was either too stupid or too clever to resent such trifles. It soon began to look as if he were by no means so stupid as he looked; for he disposed of Harker's eager questions in a manner that was slow but methodical and rational.

'Well,' said Harker (his head full of many manuals with titles like 'Be a Detective in Ten Days'). 'Well, it's the old triangle, I suppose. Accident, Suicide or Murder.'

'I don't see how it could be accident,' answered the policeman. 'It wasn't even dark yet and the pool's fifty yards from the straight road that he knew like his own doorstep. He'd no more have got into that pond than he'd go and carefully lie down in a puddle in the street. As for suicide, it's rather a responsibility to suggest it, and rather improbable too. The Admiral was a pretty spry and successful man and frightfully rich, nearly a millionaire in fact; though of course that doesn't prove anything. He seemed to be pretty normal and comfortable in his private life too; he's the last man I should suspect of drowning himself.'

'So that we come,' said the secretary, lowering his voice with the thrill, 'I suppose we come to the third possibility.'

'We won't be in too much of a hurry about that,' said the Inspector to the annoyance of Harker, who was in a hurry about everything. 'But naturally there are one or two things one would like to know. One would like to know about his property, for instance. Do you know who's likely to come in for it? You're his private secretary; do you know anything about his will?'

'I'm not so private a secretary as all that,' answered the young man. 'His solicitors are Messrs Willis, Hardman and Dyke, over in Suttford High Street; and I believe the will is in their custody.'

'Well, I'd better get round and see them pretty soon,' said the Inspector.

'Let's get round and see them at once,' said the impatient secretary.

He took a turn or two restlessly up and down the room and then exploded in a fresh place.

'What have you done about the body, Inspector?' he asked.

'Dr Straker is examining it now at the Police Station. His report ought to be ready in an hour or so.'

'It can't be ready too soon,' said Harker. 'It would save time if we could meet him at the lawyer's.' Then he stopped and his impetuous tone changed abruptly to one of some embarrassment.

'Look here,' he said, 'I want ... we want to consider the young lady, the poor Admiral's daughter, as much as possible just now. She's got a notion that may be all nonsense; but I wouldn't like to disappoint her. There's some friend of hers she wants to consult, staying in the town at present. Man of the name of Brown; priest or parson of some sort; she's given me his address. I don't take much stock in priests or parsons, but –'

The Inspector nodded. 'I don't take any stock in priests or parsons; but I take a lot of stock in Father Brown,' he said. 'I happened to have to do with him in a queer sort of society jewel case. He ought to have been a policeman instead of a parson.'

'Oh, all right,' said the breathless secretary as he vanished from the room. 'Let him come to the lawyer's too.'

Thus it happened that, when they hurried across to the neighbouring town to meet Dr Straker at the solicitor's office, they found Father Brown already seated there, with his hands folded on his heavy umbrella, chatting pleasantly to the only available member of the firm. Dr Straker also had arrived, but apparently only at that moment, as he was carefully placing his gloves in his top-hat and his top-hat on a side-table. And the mild and beaming expression of the priest's moonlike face and spectacles, together with the silent chuckles of the jolly old grizzled lawyer, to whom he was talking, were enough to show that the doctor had not yet opened his mouth to bring the news of death.

'A beautiful morning after all,' Father Brown was saying. 'That storm seems to have passed over us. There were some big black clouds, but I notice that not a drop of rain fell.'

'Not a drop,' agreed the solicitor toying with a pen; he was the third partner, Mr Dyke; 'there's not a cloud in the sky now. It's the sort of day for a holiday.' Then he realized the newcomers and looked up, laying down the pen and rising. 'Ah, Mr Harker, how are you? I hear the Admiral is expected home soon.' Then Harker spoke, and his voice rang hollow in the room.

'I am sorry to say we are the bearers of bad news. Admiral Craven was drowned before reaching home.'

There was a change in the very air of the still office, though not in the attitudes of the motionless figures; both were staring at the speaker as if a joke had been frozen on their lips. Both repeated the word 'drowned' and looked at each other, and then again at their informant. Then there was a small hubbub of questions.

'When did this happen?' asked the priest.

'Where was he found?' asked the lawyer.

'He was found,' said the Inspector, 'in that pool by the coast, not far from the Green Man, and dragged out all covered with green scum and weeds so as to be almost unrecognizable. But Dr Straker here has – What is the matter, Father Brown? Are you ill?'

'The Green Man,' said Father Brown with a shudder. 'I'm so sorry . . . I beg your pardon for being upset.'

'Upset by what?' asked the staring officer.

'By his being covered with green scum, I suppose,' said the priest, with a rather shaky laugh. Then he added rather more firmly, 'I thought it might have been seaweed.'

By this time everybody was looking at the priest, with a not unnatural suspicion that he was mad; and yet the next crucial surprise was not to come from him. After a dead silence, it was the doctor who spoke.

Dr Straker was a remarkable man, even to look at. He was very tall and angular, formal and professional in his dress; yet retaining a fashion that has hardly been known since Mid-Victorian times. Though comparatively young, he wore his brown beard, very long and spreading over his waistcoat; in contrast with it, his features, which were both harsh and handsome, looked singularly pale. His good looks were also diminished by something in his deep eyes that was not squinting, but like the shadow of a squint.

Everybody noticed these things about him, because the moment he spoke, he gave forth an indescribable air of authority. But all he said was:

'There is one more thing to be said, if you come to details, about Admiral Craven being drowned.' Then he added reflectively, 'Admiral Craven was not drowned.'

The Inspector turned with quite a new promptitude and shot a question at him.

'I have just examined the body,' said Dr Straker, 'the cause of death was a stab through the heart with some pointed blade like a stiletto. It was after death, and even some little time after, that the body was hidden in the pool.'

Father Brown was regarding Dr Straker with a very lively eye, such as he seldom turned upon anybody; and when the group in the office began to break up, he managed to attach himself to the medical man for a little further conversation, as they went back down the street. There had not been very much else to detain them except the rather formal question of the will. The impatience of the young secretary had been somewhat tried by the professional etiquette of the old lawyer. But the latter was ultimately induced, rather by the tact of the priest than the authority of the policeman, to refrain from making a mystery where there was no mystery at all. Mr Dyke admitted, with a smile, that the Admiral's will was a very normal and ordinary document, leaving everything to his only child Olive; and that there really was no particular reason for concealing the fact.

The doctor and the priest walked slowly down the street that struck out of the town in the direction of Craven House. Harker had plunged on ahead of him with all his native eagerness to get somewhere; but the two behind seemed more interested in their discussion than their direction. It was in rather an enigmatic tone that the tall doctor said to the short cleric beside him:

'Well, Father Brown, what do you think of a thing like this?'

Father Brown looked at him rather intently for an instant and then said: 'Well, I've begun to think of one or two things; but my chief difficulty is that I only knew the Admiral slightly; though I've seen something of his daughter.'

'The Admiral,' said the doctor with a grim immobility of

feature, 'was the sort of man of whom it is said that he had not an enemy in the world.'

'I suppose you mean,' answered the priest, 'that there's something else that will not be said.'

'Oh, it's no affair of mine,' said Straker hastily but rather harshly. 'He had his moods, I suppose. He once threatened me with a legal action about an operation; but I think he thought better of it. I can imagine his being rather rough with a subordinate.'

Father Brown's eyes were fixed on the figure of the secretary striding far ahead; and as he gazed he realized the special cause of his hurry. Some fifty yards farther ahead the Admiral's daughter was dawdling along the road towards the Admiral's house. The secretary soon came abreast of her; and for the remainder of the time Father Brown watched the silent drama of two human backs as they diminished into the distance. The secretary was evidently very much excited about something; but if the priest guessed what it was, he kept it to himself. When he came to the corner leading to the doctor's house, he only said briefly: 'I don't know if you have anything more to tell us.'

'Why should I?' answered the doctor very abruptly; and striding off, left it uncertain whether he was asking why he should have anything to tell, or why he should tell it.

Father Brown went stumping on alone, in the track of the two young people; but when he came to the entrance and avenues of the Admiral's park, he was arrested by the action of the girl, who turned suddenly and came straight towards him; her face unusually pale and her eyes bright with some new and as yet nameless emotion.

'Father Brown,' she said in a low voice, 'I must talk to you as soon as possible. You must listen to me, I can't see any other way out.'

'Why certainly,' he replied, as coolly as if a gutter-boy had asked him the time. 'Where shall we go and talk?'

The girl led him at random to one of the rather tumbledown arbours in the grounds; and they sat down behind a screen of large ragged leaves. She began instantly, as if she must relieve her feelings or faint.

'Harold Harker,' she said, 'has been talking to me about things. Terrible things.'

The priest nodded and the girl went on hastily. 'About Roger Rook. Do you know about Roger?'

'I've been told,' he answered, 'that his fellow-seamen call him The Jolly Roger, because he is never jolly; and looks like the pirate's skull and crossbones.'

'He was not always like that,' said Olive in a low voice. 'Something very queer must have happened to him. I knew him well when we were children; we used to play over there on the sands. He was harum-scarum and always talking about being a pirate; I dare say he was the sort they say might take to crime through reading shockers; but there was something poetical in his way of being piratical. He really was a Jolly Roger then. I suppose he was the last boy who kept up the old legend of really running away to sea; and at last his family had to agree to his joining the Navy. Well . . .'

'Yes,' said Father Brown patiently.

'Well,' she admitted, caught in one of her rare moments of mirth, 'I suppose poor Roger found it disappointing. Naval officers so seldom carry knives in their teeth or wave bloody cutlasses and black flags. But that doesn't explain the change in him. He just stiffened; grew dull and dumb, like a dead man walking about. He always avoids me; but that doesn't matter. I supposed some great grief that's no business of mine had broken him up. And now – well, if what Harold says is true, the grief is neither more nor less than going mad; or being possessed of a devil.'

'And what does Harold say?' asked the priest.

'It's so awful I can hardly say it,' she answered. 'He swears he saw Roger creeping behind my father that night; hesitating and then drawing his sword . . . and the doctor says father was stabbed with a steel point . . . I *can't* believe Roger Rook had anything to do with it. His sulks and my father's temper sometimes led to quarrels; but what are quarrels? I can't exactly say I'm standing up for an old friend; because he isn't even friendly. But you can't help feeling sure of some things, even about an old acquaintance. And yet Harold swears that he –'

'Harold seems to swear a great deal,' said Father Brown.

There was a sudden silence; after which she said in a different tone:

'Well, he does swear other things too. Harold Harker proposed to me just now.'

'Am I to congratulate you, or rather him?' inquired her companion.

'I told him he must wait. He isn't good at waiting.' She was caught again in a ripple of her incongruous sense of the comic: 'He said I was his ideal and his ambition and so on. He has lived in the States; but somehow I never remember it when he is talking about dollars; only when he is talking about ideals.'

'And I suppose,' said Father Brown very softly, 'that it is because you have to decide about Harold that you want to know the truth about Roger.'

She stiffened and frowned, and then equally abruptly smiled, saying: 'Oh, you know too much.'

'I know very little, especially in this affair,' said the priest gravely. 'I only know who murdered your father.' She started up and stood staring down at him stricken white. Father Brown made a wry face as he went on: 'I made a fool of myself when I first realized it; when they'd just been asking where he was found, and went on talking about green scum and the Green Man.'

Then he also rose; clutching his clumsy umbrella with a new resolution, he addressed the girl with a new gravity.

'There is something else that I know, which is the key to all these riddles of yours; but I won't tell you yet. I suppose it's bad news; but it's nothing like so bad as the things you have been fancying.' He buttoned up his coat and turned towards the gate. 'I'm going to see this Mr Rook of yours. In a shed by the shore, near where Mr Harker saw him walking. I rather think he lives there.' And he went bustling off in the direction of the beach.

Olive was an imaginative person; perhaps too imaginative to be safely left to brood over such hints as her friend had thrown out; but he was in rather a hurry to find the best relief for her broodings. The mysterious connection between Father Brown's first shock of enlightenment and the chance language about the pool and the inn, hag-rode her fancy in a hundred forms of ugly symbolism. The Green Man became a ghost trailing loathsome weeds and walking the countryside under the moon; the sign of the Green Man became a human figure hanging as from a gibbet; and the tarn itself became a tavern, a dark subaqueous tavern for the dead sailors. And yet he had taken the most rapid method to overthrow all such nightmares, with a burst of blinding daylight which seemed more mysterious than the night.

For before the sun had set, something had come back into her life that turned her whole world topsy-turvy once more; something she had hardly known that she desired until it was abruptly granted; something that was, like a dream, old and familiar, and yet remained incomprehensible and incredible. For Roger Rook had come striding across the sands, and even when he was a dot in the distance, she knew he was transfigured; and as he came nearer and nearer, she saw that his dark face was alive with laughter and exultation. He came straight towards her, as if they had never parted, and seized her shoulders saying: 'Now I can look after you, thank God.'

She hardly knew what she answered; but she heard herself questioning rather wildly why he seemed so changed and so happy.

'Because I am happy,' he answered. 'I have heard the bad news.'

All parties concerned, including some who seemed rather unconcerned, found themselves assembled on the garden-path leading to Craven House, to hear the formality, now truly formal, of the lawyer's reading of the will; and the probable, and more practical, sequel of the lawyer's advice upon the crisis. Besides the grey-haired solicitor himself, armed with the testamentary document, there was the Inspector armed with more direct authority touching the crime, and Lieutenant Rook in undisguised attendance on the lady; some were rather mystified on seeing the tall figure of the doctor, some smiled a little on seeing the dumpy figure of the priest. Mr Harker, that Flying Mercury, had shot down to the lodge-gates to meet them, led them back on to the lawn, and then dashed ahead of them again to prepare their reception. He said he would be back in a jiffy; and anyone observing his piston-rod of energy could well believe it; but, for the moment, they were left rather stranded on the lawn outside the house.

'Reminds me of somebody making runs at cricket,' said the Lieutenant.

'That young man,' said the lawyer, 'is rather annoyed that the law cannot move quite so quickly as he does. Fortunately Miss Craven understands our professional difficulties and delays. She has kindly assured me that she still has confidence in my slowness.'

'I wish,' said the doctor, suddenly, 'that I had as much confidence in his quickness.'

'Why, what do you mean?' asked Rook, knitting his brows; 'do you mean that Harker is too quick?'

'Too quick and too slow,' said Dr Straker, in his rather cryptic fashion. 'I know one occasion at least when he was not so very quick. Why was he hanging about half the night by the pond and the Green Man, before the Inspector came down and found the body? Why did he meet the Inspector? Why should he expect to meet the Inspector outside the Green Man?'

'I don't understand you,' said Rook. 'Do you mean that Harker wasn't telling the truth?'

Dr Straker was silent. The grizzled lawyer laughed with grim good humour.

'I have nothing more serious to say against the young man,' he said, 'than that he made a prompt and praiseworthy attempt to teach me my own business.'

'For that matter, he made an attempt to teach me mine,' said the Inspector, who had just joined the group in front. 'But that doesn't matter. If Dr Straker means anything by his hints, they do matter. I must ask you to speak plainly, doctor. It may be my duty to question him at once.'

'Well, here he comes,' said Rook, as the alert figure of the secretary appeared once more in the doorway.

At this point Father Brown, who had remained silent and inconspicuous at the tail of the procession, astonished everybody very much; perhaps especially those who knew him. He not only walked rapidly to the front, but turned facing the whole group with an arresting and almost threatening expression, like a sergeant bringing soldiers to the halt.

'Stop!' he said almost sternly. 'I apologize to everybody; but it's absolutely necessary that I should see Mr Harker first. I've got to tell him something I know; and I don't think anybody else knows; something he's got to hear. It may save a very tragic misunderstanding with somebody later on.'

'What on earth do you mean?' asked old Dyke the lawyer.

'I mean the bad news,' said Father Brown.

'Here, I say,' began the Inspector indignantly; and then suddenly caught the priest's eye and remembered strange things he had seen in other days. 'Well, if it were anyone in the world but you I should say of all the infernal cheek –'

But Father Brown was already out of hearing, and a moment afterwards was plunged in talk with Harker in the porch. They walked to and fro together for a few paces and then disappeared into the dark interior. It was about twelve minutes afterwards that Father Brown came out alone.

To their surprise he showed no disposition to re-enter the house, now that the whole company were at last about to enter it. He threw himself down on the rather rickety seat in the leafy arbour, and as the procession disappeared through the doorway, lit a pipe and proceeded to stare vacantly at the long ragged leaves about his head and to listen to the birds. There was no man who had a more hearty and enduring appetite for doing nothing.

He was apparently in a cloud of smoke and a dream of abstraction, when the front doors were once more flung open and two or three figures came out helter-skelter, running towards him, the daughter of the house and her young admirer Mr Rook being easily winners in the race. Their faces were alight with astonishment; and the face of Inspector Burns, who advanced more heavily behind them, like an elephant shaking the garden, was inflamed with some indignation as well.

'What *can* all this mean?' cried Olive, as she came panting to a halt. 'He's gone!'

'Bolted!' said the Lieutenant explosively. 'Harker's just

managed to pack a suitcase and bolted! Gone clean out of the back door and over the garden-wall to God knows where. What *did* you say to him?'

'Don't be silly!' said Olive, with a more worried expression. 'Of course you told him you'd found him out, and now he's gone. I never could have believed he was wicked like that!'

'Well!' gasped the Inspector, bursting into their midst. 'What have you done now? What have you let me down like this for?'

'Well,' repeated Father Brown, 'what have I done?'

'You have let a murderer escape,' cried Burns, with a decision that was like a thunderclap in the quiet garden; 'you have *helped* a murderer to escape. Like a fool I let you warn him; and now he is miles away.'

'I have helped a few murderers in my time, it is true,' said Father Brown; then he added, in careful distinction, 'not, you will understand, helped them to commit the murder.'

'But you knew all the time,' insisted Olive. 'You guessed from the first that it must be he. That's what you meant about being upset by the business of finding the body. That's what the doctor meant by saying my father might be disliked by a subordinate.'

'That's what I complain of,' said the official indignantly. 'You knew even then that he was the –'

'You knew even then,' insisted Olive, 'that the murderer was –'

Father Brown nodded gravely. 'Yes,' he said. 'I knew even then that the murderer was old Dyke.'

'Was *who*?' repeated the Inspector and stopped amid a dead silence; punctuated only by the occasional pipe of birds.

'I mean Mr Dyke, the solicitor,' explained Father Brown, like one explaining something elementary to an infant class. 'That gentleman with grey hair who's supposed to be going to read the will.'

They all stood like statues staring at him, as he carefully filled his pipe again and struck a match. At last Burns rallied his vocal powers to break the strangling silence with an effort resembling violence.

'But, in the name of heaven, *why*?'

'Ah, why?' said the priest and rose thoughtfully, puffing at his pipe. 'As to why he did it ... Well, I suppose the time has come to tell you, or those of you who don't know, the fact that is the key of all this business. It's a great calamity; and it's a great crime; but it's not the murder of Admiral Craven.'

He looked Olive full in the face and said very seriously:

'I tell you the bad news bluntly and in few words; because I think you are brave enough, and perhaps happy enough, to take it well. You have the chance, and I think the power, to be something like a great woman. You are not a great heiress.'

Amid the silence that followed it was he who resumed his explanation.

'Most of your father's money, I am sorry to say, has gone. It went by the financial dexterity of the grey-haired gentleman named Dyke, who is (I grieve to say) a swindler. Admiral Craven was murdered to silence him about the way in which he was swindled. The fact that he was ruined and you were disinherited is the single simple clue, not only to the murder, but to all the other mysteries in this business.' He took a puff or two and then continued.

'I told Mr Rook you were disinherited and he rushed back to help you. Mr Rook is a rather remarkable person.'

'Oh, chuck it,' said Mr Rook with a hostile air.

'Mr Rook is a monster,' said Father Brown with scientific calm. 'He is an anachronism, an atavism, a brute survival of the Stone Age. If there was one barbarous superstition we all supposed to be utterly extinct and dead in these days, it was that notion about honour and independence. But then I get mixed up with so many dead superstitions. Mr Rook is an extinct animal. He is a plesiosaurus. He did not want to live on his wife or have a wife who could call him a fortune-hunter. Therefore he sulked in a grotesque manner and only came to life again when I brought him the good news that you were ruined. He wanted to work for his wife and not be kept by her. Disgusting, isn't it? Let us turn to the brighter topic of Mr Harker.

'I told Mr Harker you were disinherited and he rushed away in a sort of panic. Do not be too hard on Mr Harker. He really had better as well as worse enthusiasms; but he had them all mixed up. There is no harm in having ambitions; but he had ambitions and called them ideals. The old sense of honour taught men to suspect success; to say, "This is a benefit; it may be a bribe." The new nine-times-accursed nonsense about Making Good teaches men to identify being good with making money. That was all that was the matter with him; in every other way he was a thoroughly good fellow, and there are thousands like him. Gazing at the stars and rising in the world were all Uplift. Marrying a good wife and marrying a rich wife were all Making Good. But he was not a cynical scoundrel; or he would simply have come back and jilted or cut you as the case might be. He could not face you; while you were there, half of his broken ideal was left.

'I did not tell the Admiral; but somebody did. Word came to him somehow, during the last grand parade on board, that his friend the family lawyer had betrayed him. He was in such a towering passion that he did what he could never have done in his senses; came straight on shore in his cocked hat and gold lace to catch the criminal; he wired to the police station, and that was why the Inspector was wandering round the Green Man. Lieutenant Rook followed him on shore because he suspected some family trouble and had half a hope he might help and put himself right. Hence his hesitating behaviour. As for his drawing his sword when he dropped behind and thought he was alone, well that's a matter of imagination. He was a romantic person who had dreamed of swords and run away to sea; and found himself in a service where he wasn't even allowed to wear a sword except about once in three years. He thought he was quite alone on the sands where he played as a boy. If you don't understand what he did, I can only say, like Stevenson, "you will never be a pirate." Also you will never be a poet; and you have never been a boy.'

'I never have,' answered Olive gravely, 'and yet I think I understand.'

'Almost every man,' continued the priest musing, 'will play with anything shaped like a sword or dagger, even if it is a paper-knife. That is why I thought it so odd when the lawyer didn't.'

'What do you mean?' asked Burns, 'didn't what?'

'Why, didn't you notice,' answered Brown, 'at that first

meeting in the office, the lawyer played with a pen and not with a paper-knife; though he had a beautiful bright steel paper-knife in the pattern of a stiletto? The pens were dusty and splashed with ink; but the knife had just been cleaned. But he did not play with it. There are limits to the irony of assassins.'

After a silence the Inspector said, like one waking from a dream: 'Look here ... I don't know whether I'm on my head or my heels; I don't know whether you think you've got to the end; but I haven't got to the beginning. Where do you get all this lawyer stuff from? What started you out on that trail?'

Father Brown laughed curtly and without mirth.

'The murderer made a slip at the start,' he said, 'and I can't think why nobody else noticed it. When you brought the first news of the death to the solicitor's office, nobody was supposed to know anything there, except that the Admiral was expected home. When you said he was drowned, I asked when it happened and Mr Dyke asked where the corpse was found.'

He paused a moment to knock out his pipe and resumed reflectively:

'Now when you are simply told of a seaman, returning from the sea, that he has been drowned, it is natural to assume that he has been drowned at sea. At any rate, to allow that he may have been drowned at sea. If he had been washed overboard, or gone down with his ship, or had his body "committed to the deep", there would be no reason to expect his body to be found at all. The moment that man asked where it was found, I was sure he knew where it was found. Because he had put it there. Nobody but the murderer need have thought of anything so unlikely as a seaman being drowned in a land-locked pool a few hundred yards from the sea. That is why I suddenly felt sick and turned green, I dare say; as green as the Green Man. I never *can* get used to finding myself suddenly sitting beside a murderer. So I had to turn it off by talking in parables; but the parable meant something, after all. I said that the body was covered with green scum, but it might just as well have been seaweed.'

It is fortunate that tragedy can never kill comedy and that the two can run side by side; and that while the only acting partner of the business of Messrs Willis, Hardman and Dyke blew his brains out when the Inspector entered the house to arrest him, Olive and Roger were calling to each other across the sands at evening, as they did when they were children together.

FIVE

The Pursuit of Mr Blue

ALONG a seaside parade on a sunny afternoon, a person with the depressing name of Muggleton was moving with suitable gloom. There was a horseshoe of worry in his forehead, and the numerous groups and strings of entertainers stretched along the beach below looked up to him in vain for applause. Pierrots turned up their pale moon faces, like the white bellies of dead fish, without improving his spirits; niggers with faces entirely grey with a sort of grimy soot were equally unsuccessful in filling his fancy with brighter things. He was a sad and disappointed man. His other features, besides the bald brow with its furrow, were retiring and almost sunken; and a certain dingy refinement about them made more incongruous the one aggressive ornament of his face. It was an outstanding and bristling military moustache; and it looked suspiciously like a false moustache. It is possible, indeed, that it was a false moustache. It is possible, on the other hand, that even if it was not false it was forced. He might almost have grown it in a hurry, by a mere act of will; so much was it a part of his job rather than his personality.

For the truth is that Mr Muggleton was a private detective in a small way, and the cloud on his brow was due to a big blunder in his professional career; anyhow it was connected with something darker than the mere possession of such a surname. He might almost, in an obscure sort of way, have been proud of his surname; for he came of poor but decent Nonconformist people who claimed some connection with the founder of the Muggletonians; the only man who had hitherto had the courage to appear with that name in human history.

The more legitimate cause of his annoyance (at least as he himself explained it) was that he had just been present at the bloody murder of a world-famous millionaire, and had failed to prevent it, though he had been engaged at a salary of five pounds a week to do so. Thus we may explain the fact that even the languorous singing of the song entitled, 'Won't You Be My Loodah Doodah Day?' failed to fill him with the joy of life.

For that matter, there were others on the beach, who might have had more sympathy with his murderous theme and Muggletonian tradition. Seaside resorts are the chosen pitches, not only of pierrots appealing to the amorous emotions, but also of preachers who often seem to specialize in a correspondingly sombre and sulphurous style of preaching. There was one aged ranter whom he could hardly help noticing, so piercing were the cries, not to say shrieks of religious prophecy that rang above all the banjos and the castanets. This was a long, loose, shambling old man, dressed in something like a fisherman's jersey; but inappropriately equipped with a pair of those very long and drooping whiskers which have never been seen since the disappearance of certain sportive Mid-Victorian dandies. As it was the custom for all mountebanks on the beach to display something, as if they were selling it, the old man displayed a rather rotten-looking fisherman's net, which he generally spread out invitingly on the sands, as if it were a carpet for queens; but occasionally whirled wildly round his head with a gesture almost as terrific as that of the Roman Retiarius, ready to impale people on a trident. Indeed, he might really have impaled people, if he had had a trident. His words were always pointed towards punishment; his hearers heard nothing except threats to the body or the soul; he was so far in the same mood as Mr Muggleton, that he might almost have been a mad hangman addressing a crowd of murderers. The boys called him Old Brimstone; but he had other eccentricities besides the purely theological. One of his eccentricities was to climb up into the nest of iron girders under the pier and trail his net in the water, declaring that he got his living by fishing; though it is doubtful whether anybody had ever seen him catching fish. Worldly trippers, however, would sometimes start at a voice in their ear, threatening judgement as from a thundercloud, but really coming from the perch under the iron roof where the old monomaniac sat glaring, his fantastic whiskers hanging like grey seaweed.

The detective, however, could have put up with Old Brimstone much better than with the other parson he was destined to meet. To explain this second and more momentous meeting, it must be pointed out that Muggleton, after his remarkable experience in the matter of the murder, had very properly put all his cards on the table. He told his story to the police and to the only available representative of Braham Bruce, the dead millionaire; that is, to his very dapper secretary, a Mr Anthony Taylor. The Inspector was more sympathetic than the secretary; but the sequel of his sympathy was the last thing Muggleton would normally have associated with police advice. The Inspector, after some reflection, very much surprised Mr Muggleton by advising him to consult an able amateur whom he knew to be staying in the town. Mr Muggleton had read reports and romances about the Great Criminologist, who sits in his library like an intellectual spider, and throws out theoretical filaments of a web as large as the world. He was prepared to be led to the lonely château where the expert wore a purple dressing-gown, to the attic where he lived on opium and acrostics, to the vast laboratory or the lonely tower. To his astonishment he was led to the very edge of the crowded beach by the pier to meet a dumpy little clergyman, with a broad hat and a broad grin, who was at that moment hopping about on the sands with a crowd of poor children; and excitedly waving a very little wooden spade.

When the criminological clergyman, whose name appeared to be Brown, had at last been detached from the children, though not from the spade, he seemed to Muggleton to grow more and more unsatisfactory. He hung about helplessly among the idiotic side-shows of the seashore, talking about random topics and particularly attaching himself to those rows of automatic machines which are set up in such places; solemnly spending penny after penny in order to play vicarious games of golf, football, cricket, conducted by clockwork figures; and finally contenting himself with the miniature exhibition of a race, in which one metal doll appeared merely to run and jump after the other. And yet all the time he was listening very carefully to the story which the defeated detective poured out to him. Only his way of not letting his right hand know what his left hand was doing, with pennies, got very much on the detective's nerves.

'Can't we go and sit down somewhere,' said Muggleton impatiently. 'I've got a letter you ought to see, if you're to know anything at all of this business.'

Father Brown turned away with a sigh from the jumping dolls, and went and sat down with his companion on an iron seat on the shore; his companion had already unfolded the letter and handed it silently to him.

It was an abrupt and queer sort of letter, Father Brown thought. He knew that millionaires did not always specialize in manners, especially in dealing with dependants like detectives; but there seemed to be something more in the letter than mere brusquerie.

DEAR MUGGLETON,

I never thought I should come down to wanting help of this sort; but I'm about through with things. It's been getting more and more intolerable for the last two years. I guess all you need to know about the story is this. There is a dirty rascal who is a cousin of mine, I'm ashamed to say. He's been a tout, a tramp, a quack doctor, an actor, and all that; even has the brass to act under our name and call himself Bertrand Bruce. I believe he's either got some potty job at the theatre here, or is looking for one. But you may take it from me that the job isn't his real job. His real job is running me down and knocking me out for good, if he can. It's an old story and no business of anybody's; there was a time when we started neck and neck and ran a race of ambition – and what they call love as well. Was it my fault that he was a rotter and I was a man who succeeds in things? But the dirty devil swears he'll succeed yet; shoot me and run off with my – never mind. I suppose he's a sort of madman, but he'll jolly soon try to be some sort of murderer.

I'll give you £5 a week if you'll meet me at the lodge at the end of the pier, just after the pier closes tonight – and take on my job. It's the only safe place to meet – if anything is safe by this time.

J. BRAHAM BRUCE

'Dear me,' said Father Brown mildly. 'Dear me. A rather hurried letter.'

Muggleton nodded; and after a pause began his own story; in an oddly refined voice contrasting with his clumsy appearance.

The priest knew well the hobbies of concealed culture hidden in many dingy lower and middle class men; but even he was startled by the excellent choice of words only a shade too pedantic; the man talked like a book.

'I arrived at the little round-house at the end of the pier before there was any sign of my distinguished client. I opened the door and went inside, feeling that he might prefer me, as well as himself, to be as inconspicuous as possible. Not that it mattered very much; for the pier was too long for anybody to have seen us from the beach or the parade, and, on glancing at my watch, I saw by the time that the pier entrance must have already closed. It was flattering, after a fashion, that he should thus ensure that we should be alone together at the rendezvous, as showing that he did really rely on my assistance or protection. Anyhow, it was his idea that we should meet on the pier after closing time, so I fell in with it readily enough. There were two chairs inside the little round pavilion, or whatever you call it; so I simply took one of them and waited. I did not have to wait long. He was famous for his punctuality, and sure enough, as I looked up at the one little round window opposite me I saw him pass slowly, as if making a preliminary circuit of the place.

'I had only seen portraits of him, and that a long time ago; and naturally he was rather older than the portraits, but there was no mistaking the likeness. The profile that passed the window was of the sort called aquiline, after the beak of the eagle; but he rather suggested a grey and venerable eagle; an eagle in repose; an eagle that has long folded its wings. There was no mistaking, however, that look of authority, or silent pride in the habit of command, that has always marked men who, like him, have organized great systems and been obeyed. He was quietly dressed, what I could see of him; especially as compared with the crowd of seaside trippers which had filled so much of my day; but I fancied his overcoat was of that extra elegant sort that is cut to follow the line of the figure, and it had a strip of astrakhan lining showing on the lapels. All this, of course, I took in at a glance, for I had already got to my feet and gone to the door. I put out my hand and received the first shock of that terrible evening. The door was locked. Somebody had locked me in.

'For a moment I stood stunned, and still staring at the round window, from which, of course, the moving profile had already passed; and then I suddenly saw the explanation. Another profile, pointed like that of a pursuing hound, flashed into the circle of vision, as into a round mirror. The moment I saw it, I knew who it was. It was the Avenger; the murderer or would-be murderer, who had trailed the old millionaire for so long across land and sea, and had now tracked him to this blind-alley of an iron pier that hung between sea and land. And I knew, of course, that it was the murderer who had locked the door.

'The man I saw first had been tall, but his pursuer was even taller; an effect that was only lessened by his carrying his shoulders hunched very high and his neck and head thrust forward like a true beast of the chase. The effect of the combination gave him rather the look of a gigantic hunchback. But something of the blood relationship that connected this ruffian with his famous kinsman showed in the two profiles as they passed across the circle of glass. The pursuer also had a nose rather like the beak of a bird; though his general air of ragged degradation suggested the vulture rather than the eagle. He was unshaven to the point of being bearded, and the humped look of his shoulders was increased by the coils of a coarse woollen scarf. All these are trivialities, and can give no impression of the ugly energy of that outline, or the sense of avenging doom in that stooping and striding figure. Have you ever seen William Blake's design, sometimes called with some levity, "The Ghost of a Flea," but also called, with somewhat greater lucidity, "A Vision of Blood Guilt," or something of that kind? That is just such a nightmare of a stealthy giant, with high shoulders, carrying a knife and bowl. This man carried neither, but as he passed the window the second time, I saw with my own eyes that he loosened a revolver from the folds of the scarf and held it gripped and poised in his hand. The eyes in his head shifted and shone in the moonlight, and that in a very creepy way; they shot forward and back with lightning leaps; almost as if he could shoot them out like luminous horns, as do certain reptiles.

'Three times the pursued and the pursuer passed in succession outside the window, treading their narrow circle, before I fully awoke to the need of some action, however desperate. I shook the door with rattling violence; when next I saw the face of the unconscious victim I beat furiously on the window; then I tried to break the window. But it was a double window of exceptionally thick glass, and so deep was the embrasure that I doubted if I could properly reach the outer window at all. Anyhow, my dignified client took no notice of my noise or signals; and the revolving shadow-pantomime of those two masks of doom continued to turn round and round me, till I felt almost dizzy as well as sick. Then they suddenly ceased to reappear. I waited; and I knew that they would not come again. I knew that the crisis had come.

'I need not tell you more. You can almost imagine the rest; even as I sat there helpless, trying to imagine it; or trying not to imagine it. It is enough to say that in that awful silence, in which all sounds of footsteps had died away, there were only two other noises besides the rumbling undertones of the sea. The first was the loud noise of a shot and the second the duller noise of a splash.

'My client had been murdered within a few yards of me, and I could make no sign. I will not trouble you with what I felt about that. But even if I could recover from the murder, I am still confronted with the mystery.'

'Yes,' said Father Brown very gently, 'which mystery?'

'The mystery of how the murderer got away,' answered the other. 'The instant people were admitted to the pier next morning, I was released from my prison and went racing back to the entrance gates, to inquire who had left the pier since they were opened. Without bothering you with details, I may explain that they were, by a rather unusual arrangement, real full-size iron doors that would keep anybody out (or in) until they were opened. The officials there had seen nobody in the least resembling the assassin returning that way. And he was a rather unmistakable person. Even if he had disguised himself somehow, he could hardly have disguised his extraordinary height or got rid of the family nose. It is extraordinarily unlikely that he tried to swim ashore, for the sea was very rough; and there are certainly no traces of any landing. And, somehow, having seen the face of that fiend even once, let alone about six times, something gives me an overwhelming conviction that he did not simply drown himself in the hour of triumph.'

'I quite understand what you mean by that,' replied Father Brown. 'Besides, it would be very inconsistent with the tone of his original threatening letter, in which he promised himself all sorts of benefits after the crime ... there's another point it might be well to verify. What about the structure of the pier underneath? Piers are very often made with a whole network of iron supports, which a man might climb through as a monkey climbs through a forest.'

'Yes, I thought of that,' replied the private investigator; 'but unfortunately this pier is oddly constructed in more ways than one. It's quite unusually long, and there are iron columns with all that tangle of iron girders; only they're very far apart and I can't see any way a man could climb from one to the other.'

'I only mentioned it,' said Father Brown thoughtfully, 'because that queer fish with the long whiskers, the old man who preaches on the sand, often climbs up on to the nearest girder. I believe he sits there fishing when the tide comes up. And he's a very queer fish to go fishing.'

'Why, what do you mean?'

'Well,' said Father Brown very slowly, twiddling with a button and gazing abstractedly out to the great green waters glittering in the last evening light after the sunset. 'Well ... I tried to talk to him in a friendly sort of way; friendly and not too funny, if you understand, about his combining the ancient trades of fishing and preaching; I think I made the obvious reference; the text that refers to fishing for living souls. And he said quite queerly and harshly, as he jumped back on to his iron perch, "Well, at least I fish for dead bodies."'

'Good God!' exclaimed the detective, staring at him.

'Yes,' said the priest. 'It seemed to me an odd remark to make in a chatty way, to a stranger playing with children on the sands.'

After another staring silence, his companion eventually ejaculated: 'You don't mean you think he had anything to do with the death.'

'I think,' answered Father Brown, 'that he might throw some light on it.'

'Well, it's beyond me now,' said the detective. 'It's beyond me to believe that anybody can throw any light on it. It's like a welter of wild waters in the pitch dark; the sort of waters that he . . . that he fell into. It's simply stark staring unreason; a big man vanishing like a bubble; nobody could possibly . . . Look here!' He stopped suddenly, staring at the priest, who had not moved, but was still twiddling with the button and staring at the breakers. 'What do you mean? What are you looking like that for? You don't mean to say that you . . . that you can make any sense of it?'

'It would be much better if it remained nonsense,' said Father Brown in a low voice. 'Well, if you ask me right out – yes, I think I can make some sense of it.'

There was a long silence, and then the inquiry agent said with a rather singular abruptness: 'Oh, here comes the old man's secretary from the hotel. I must be off. I think I'll go and talk to that mad fisherman of yours.'

'*Post hoc propter hoc*?' asked the priest with a smile.

'Well,' said the other, with jerky candour, 'the secretary don't like me and I don't think I like him. He's been poking round with a lot of questions that didn't seem to me to get us any further, except towards a quarrel. Perhaps he's jealous because the old man called in somebody else, and wasn't content with his elegant secretary's advice. See you later.'

And he turned away, ploughing through the sand to the place where the eccentric preacher had already mounted his marine nest; and looked in the green gloaming rather like some huge polyp or stinging jelly-fish trailing his poisonous filaments in the phosphorescent sea.

Meanwhile the priest was serenely watching the serene approach of the secretary; conspicuous even from afar, in that popular crowd, by the clerical neatness and sobriety of his top-hat and tail-coat. Without feeling disposed to take part in any feud between the secretary and the inquiry agent, Father Brown had a faint feeling of irrational sympathy with the prejudices of the latter. Mr Anthony Taylor, the secretary, was an extremely presentable young man, in countenance as well as costume; and the countenance was firm and intellectual as well as merely good-looking. He was pale, with dark hair coming down on the sides of his head, as if pointing towards possible whiskers; he kept his lips compressed more tightly than most people. The only thing that Father Brown's fancy could tell itself in justification sounded queerer than it really looked. He had a notion that the man talked with his nostrils. Anyhow, the strong compression of his mouth brought out something abnormally sensitive and flexible in these movements at the sides of his nose, so that he seemed to be communicating and conducting life by snuffling and smelling, with his head up, as does a dog. It somehow fitted in with the other features that, when he did speak, it was with a sudden rattling rapidity like a gatling-gun, which sounded almost ugly from so smooth and polished a figure.

For once he opened the conversation, by saying: 'No bodies washed ashore, I imagine.'

'None have been announced, certainly,' said Father Brown.

'No gigantic body of the murderer with the woollen scarf,' said Mr Taylor.

'No,' said Father Brown.

Mr Taylor's mouth did not move any more for the moment; but his nostrils spoke for him with such quick and quivering scorn, that they might almost have been called talkative.

When he did speak again, after some polite commonplaces from the priest, it was to say curtly: 'Here comes the Inspector; I suppose they've been scouring England for the scarf.'

Inspector Grinstead, a brown-faced man with a grey pointed beard, addressed Father Brown rather more respectfully than the secretary had done.

'I thought you would like to know, sir,' he said, 'that there is absolutely no trace of the man described as having escaped from the pier.'

'Or rather not described as having escaped from the pier,'

said Taylor. 'The pier officials, the only people who could have described him, have never seen anybody to describe.'

'Well,' said the Inspector, 'we've telephoned all the stations and watched all the roads, and it will be almost impossible for him to escape from England. It really seems to me as if he couldn't have got out that way. He doesn't seem to be anywhere.'

'He never was anywhere,' said the secretary, with an abrupt grating voice, that sounded like a gun going off on that lonely shore.

The Inspector looked blank; but a light dawned gradually on the face of the priest, who said at last with almost ostentatious unconcern:

'Do you mean that the man was a myth? Or possibly a lie?'

'Ah,' said the secretary, inhaling through his haughty nostrils, 'you've thought of that at last.'

'I thought of that at first,' said Father Brown. 'It's the first thing anybody would think of, isn't it, hearing an unsupported story from a stranger about a strange murderer on a lonely pier. In plain words, you mean that little Muggleton never heard anybody murdering the millionaire. Possibly you mean that little Muggleton murdered him himself.'

'Well,' said the secretary, 'Muggleton looks a dingy down-and-out sort of cove to me. There's no story but his about what happened on the pier, and his story consists of a giant who vanished; quite a fairy-tale. It isn't a very creditable tale, even as he tells it. By his own account, he bungled his case and let his patron be killed a few yards away. He's a pretty rotten fool and failure, on his own confession.'

'Yes,' said Father Brown. 'I'm rather fond of people who are fools and failures on their own confession.'

'I don't know what you mean,' snapped the other.

'Perhaps,' said Father Brown, wistfully, 'it's because so many people are fools and failures without any confession.'

Then, after a pause, he went on: 'But even if he is a fool and a failure, that doesn't prove he is a liar and a murderer. And you've forgotten that there is one piece of external evidence that does really support his story. I mean the letter from the millionaire, telling the whole tale of his cousin and his vendetta. Unless you can prove that the document itself is actually a forgery, you have to admit there was some probability of Bruce being pursued by somebody who had a real motive. Or rather, I should say, the one actually admitted and recorded motive.'

'I'm not quite sure that I understand you,' said the Inspector, 'about the motive.'

'My dear fellow,' said Father Brown, for the first time stung by impatience into familiarity, 'everybody's got a motive in a way. Considering the way that Bruce made his money, considering the way that most millionaires make their money, almost anybody in the world might have done such a perfectly natural thing as throw him into the sea. In many, one might almost fancy, it would be almost automatic. To almost all it must have occurred at some time or other. Mr Taylor might have done it.'

'What's that?' snapped Mr Taylor, and his nostrils swelled visibly.

'I might have done it,' went on Father Brown, *'nisi me constringeret ecclesiae auctoritas.* Anybody, but for the one true morality, might be tempted to accept so obvious, so simple a social solution. I might have done it; you might have done it; the Mayor or the muffin-man might have done it. The only person on this earth I can think of, who probably would not have done it, is the private inquiry agent whom Bruce had just engaged at five pounds a week, and who hadn't yet had any of his money.'

The secretary was silent for a moment; then he snorted and said: 'If that's the offer in the letter, we'd certainly better see whether it's a forgery. For really, we don't know that the whole tale isn't as false as a forgery. The fellow admits himself that the disappearance of his hunch-backed giant is utterly incredible and inexplicable.'

'Yes,' said Father Brown; 'that's what I like about Muggleton. He admits things.'

'All the same,' insisted Taylor, his nostrils vibrant with excitement. 'All the same, the long and the short of it is that he can't prove that his tall man in the scarf ever existed or does exist; and every single fact found by the police and the witnesses proves that he does not exist. No, Father Brown. There is only one way in which you can justify this little scallywag you seem to be so fond of. And that is by producing his Imaginary Man. And that is exactly what you can't do.'

'By the way,' said the priest, absentmindedly, 'I suppose you come from the hotel where Bruce has rooms, Mr Taylor?'

Taylor looked a little taken aback, and seemed almost to stammer. 'Well, he always did have those rooms; and they're practically his. I haven't actually seen him there this time.'

'I suppose you motored down with him,' observed Brown; 'or did you both come by train?'

'I came by train and brought the luggage,' said the secretary impatiently. 'Something kept him, I suppose. I haven't actually seen him since he left Yorkshire on his own a week or two ago.'

'So it seems,' said the priest very softly, 'that if Muggleton wasn't the last to see Bruce by the wild sea-waves, you were the last to see him, on the equally wild Yorkshire moors.'

Taylor had turned quite white, but he forced his grating voice to composure: 'I never said Muggleton didn't see *Bruce* on the pier.'

'No; and why didn't you?' asked Father Brown. 'If he made up one man on the pier, why shouldn't he make up two men on the pier? Of course we do know that Bruce did exist; but we don't seem to know what has happened to him for several weeks. Perhaps he was left behind in Yorkshire.'

The rather strident voice of the secretary rose almost to a scream. All his veneer of society suavity seemed to have vanished.

'You're simply shuffling! You're simply shirking! You're trying to drag in mad insinuations about me, simply because you can't answer my question.'

'Let me see,' said Father Brown reminiscently. 'What was your question?'

'You know well enough what it was; and you know you're damned well stumped by it. Where is the man with the scarf? Who has seen him? Whoever heard of him or spoke of him, except that little liar of yours? If you want to convince us, you must produce him. If he ever existed, he may be hiding in the Hebrides or off to Callao. But you've got to produce him, though I know he doesn't exist. Well then! Where is he?'

'I rather think he is over there,' said Father Brown, peering and blinking towards the nearer waves that washed round the iron pillars of the pier; where the two figures of the agent and the old fisher and preacher were still dark against the green glow of the water. 'I mean in that sort of net thing that's tossing about in the sea.'

With whatever bewilderment, Inspector Grinstead took the upper hand again with a flash, and strode down the beach.

'Do you mean to say,' he cried, 'that the murderer's body is in the old boy's net?'

Father Brown nodded as he followed down the shingly slope; and, even as they moved, little Muggleton the agent turned and began to climb the same shore, his mere dark outline a pantomime of amazement and discovery.

'It's true, for all we said,' he gasped. 'The murderer did try to swim ashore and was drowned, of course, in that weather. Or else he did really commit suicide. Anyhow, he drifted dead into Old Brimstone's fishing-net, and that's what the old maniac meant when he said he fished for dead men.'

The Inspector ran down the shore with an agility that outstripped them all, and was heard shouting out orders. In a few moments the fishermen and a few bystanders, assisted by the policemen, had hauled the net into shore, and rolled it with its burden on to the wet sands that still reflected the sunset. The secretary looked at what lay on the sands and the words died on his lips. For what lay on the sands was indeed the body of a gigantic man in rags, with huge shoulders somewhat humped and bony eagle face; and a great red ragged woollen scarf or comforter, sprawled along the sunset sands like a great stain of blood. But Taylor was staring not at the gory scarf or the fabulous stature, but at the face; and his own face was a conflict of incredulity and suspicion.

The Inspector instantly turned to Muggleton with a new air of civility.

'This certainly confirms your story,' he said. And until he heard the tone of those words, Muggleton had never guessed how almost universally his story had been disbelieved. Nobody had believed him. Nobody but Father Brown.

Therefore, seeing Father Brown edging away from the group, he made a movement to depart in his company; but even then he was brought up rather short by the discovery that the priest was once more being drawn away by the deadly attractions of the funny little automatic machines. He even saw the reverend gentleman fumbling for a penny. He stopped, however, with the penny poised in his finger and thumb, as the secretary spoke for the last time in his loud discordant voice.

'And I suppose we may add,' he said, 'that the monstrous and imbecile charges against me are also at an end.'

'My dear sir,' said the priest, 'I never made any charges against you. I'm not such a fool as to suppose you were likely to murder your master in Yorkshire and then come down here to fool about with his luggage. All I said was that I could make out a better case against you than you were making out so vigorously against poor Mr Muggleton. All the same, if you really want to learn the truth about this business (and I assure you the truth isn't generally grasped yet), I can give you a hint even from your own affairs. It *is* rather a rum and significant thing that Mr Bruce the millionaire had been unknown to all his usual haunts and habits for weeks before he was really killed. As you seem to be a promising amateur detective, I advise you to work on that line.'

'What do you mean?' asked Taylor sharply.

But he got no answer out of Father Brown, who was once more completely concentrated on jiggling the little handle of the machine, that made one doll jump out and then another doll jump after it.

'Father Brown,' said Muggleton, his old annoyance faintly reviving: 'Will you tell me why you like that fool thing so much?'

'For one reason,' replied the priest, peering closely into the glass puppet-show. 'Because it contains the secret of this tragedy.'

Then he suddenly straightened himself and looked quite seriously at his companion.

'I knew all along,' he said, 'that you were telling the truth and the opposite of the truth.'

Muggleton could only stare at a return of all the riddles.

'It's quite simple,' added the priest, lowering his voice. 'That corpse with the scarlet scarf over there is the corpse of Braham Bruce the millionaire. There won't be any other.'

'But the two men –' began Muggleton, and his mouth fell open.

'Your description of the two men was quite admirably vivid,' said Father Brown. 'I assure you I'm not at all likely to forget it. If I may say so, you have a literary talent; perhaps journalism would give you more scope than detection. I believe I remember practically each point about each person. Only, you see, queerly enough, each point affected you in one way and me in exactly the opposite way. Let's begin with the first you mentioned. You said that the first man you saw had an indescribable air of authority and dignity. And you said to yourself, "That's the Trust Magnate, the great merchant prince, the ruler of markets." But when I heard about the air of dignity and authority, I said to myself, "That's the actor; everything about him is the actor." You don't get that look by being President of the Chain Store Amalgamation Company. You get that look by being Hamlet's Father's Ghost, or Julius Caesar, or King Lear, and you never altogether lose it. You couldn't see enough of his clothes to tell whether they were really seedy, but you saw a strip of fur and a sort of faintly fashionable cut; and I said to myself again, "The actor." Next, before we go into details about the other man, notice one thing about him evidently absent from the first man. You said the second man was not only ragged but unshaven to the point of being bearded. Now we have all seen shabby actors, dirty actors, drunken actors, utterly disreputable actors. But such a thing as a scrub-bearded actor, in a job or even looking round for a job, has scarcely been seen in this world. On the other hand, shaving is often almost the first thing to go, with a gentleman or a wealthy eccentric who is really letting himself go to pieces. Now we have every reason to believe that your friend the millionaire was letting himself go to pieces. His letter was the letter of a man who had already gone to pieces. But it wasn't only negligence that made him look poor and shabby. Don't you understand that the man was practically in hiding? That was why he didn't go to his hotel; and his own secretary hadn't seen him for weeks. He was a millionaire; but his whole object was

97

to be a completely disguised millionaire. Have you ever read "The Woman in White"? Don't you remember that the fashionable and luxurious Count Fosco, fleeing for his life before a secret society, was found stabbed in the blue blouse of a common French workman? Then let us go back for a moment to the demeanour of these men. You saw the first man calm and collected and you said to yourself, "That's the innocent victim"; though the innocent victim's own letter wasn't at all calm and collected. I heard he was calm and collected; and I said to myself, "That's the murderer." Why should he be anything else but calm and collected? He knew what he was going to do. He had made up his mind to do it for a long time; if he had ever had any hesitation or remorse he had hardened himself against them before he came on the scene – in his case, we might say, on the stage. He wasn't likely to have any particular stage-fright. He didn't pull out his pistol and wave it about; why should he? He kept it in his pocket till he wanted it; very likely he fired from his pocket. The other man fidgeted with his pistol because he was as nervous as a cat, and very probably had never had a pistol before. He did it for the same reason that he rolled his eyes; and I remember that, even in your own unconscious evidence, it is particularly stated that he rolled them *backwards*. In fact, he was looking behind him. In fact, he was not the pursuer but the pursued. But because you happened to see the first man first, you couldn't help thinking of the other man as coming up behind him. In mere mathematics and mechanics, each of them was running after the other – just like the others.'

'What others?' inquired the dazed detective.

'Why, these,' cried Father Brown, striking the automatic machine with the little wooden spade, which had incongruously remained in his hand throughout these murderous mysteries. 'These little clockwork dolls that chase each other round and round for ever. Let us call them Mr Blue and Mr Red, after the colour of their coats. I happened to start off with Mr Blue, and so the children said that Mr Red was running after him; but it would have looked exactly the contrary if I had started with Mr Red.'

'Yes, I begin to see,' said Muggleton; 'and I suppose all the rest fits in. The family likeness, of course, cuts both ways, and they never saw the murderer leaving the pier –'

'They never looked for the murderer leaving the pier,' said the other. 'Nobody told them to look for a quiet clean-shaven gentleman in an astrakhan coat. All the mystery of his vanishing revolved on your description of a hulking fellow in a red neck-cloth. But the simple truth was that the actor in the astrakhan coat murdered the millionaire with the red rag, and there is the poor fellow's body. It's just like the red and blue dolls; only, because you saw one first, you guessed wrong about which was red with vengeance and which was blue with funk.'

At this point two or three children began to straggle across the sands, and the priest waved them to him with the wooden spade, theatrically tapping the automatic machine. Muggleton guessed that it was mainly to prevent their straying towards the horrible heap on the shore.

'One more penny left in the world,' said Father Brown, 'and then we must go home to tea. Do you know, Doris, I rather like those revolving games, that just go round and round like the Mulberry-Bush. After all, God made all the suns and stars to play Mulberry-Bush. But those other games, where one must catch up with another, where runners are rivals and run neck and neck and outstrip each other; well – much nastier things seem to happen. I like to think of Mr Red and Mr Blue always jumping with undiminished spirits; all free and equal; and never hurting each other. "Fond lover, never, never, wilt thou kiss – or kill." Happy, happy Mr Red!

> He cannot change; though thou hast not thy bliss,
> For ever wilt thou jump; and he be Blue.

Reciting this remarkable quotation from Keats, with some emotion, Father Brown tucked the little spade under one arm, and giving a hand to two of the children, stumped solemnly up the beach to tea.

SIX

The Crime of the Communist

THREE men came out from under the low-browed Tudor arch in the mellow façade of Mandeville College, into the strong evening sunlight of a summer day which seemed as if it would never end; and in that sunlight they saw something that blasted like lightning; well-fitted to be the shock of their lives.

Even before they had realized anything in the way of a catastrophe, they were conscious of a contrast. They themselves, in a curious quiet way, were quite harmonious with their surroundings. Though the Tudor arches that ran like a cloister round the College gardens had been built four hundred years ago, at that moment when the Gothic fell from heaven and bowed, or almost crouched, over the cosier chambers of Humanism and the Revival of Learning – though they themselves were in modern clothes (that is in clothes whose ugliness would have amazed any of the four centuries) yet something in the spirit of the place made them all at one. The gardens had been tended so carefully as to achieve the final triumph of looking careless; the very flowers seemed beautiful by accident, like elegant weeds; and the modern costumes had at least any picturesqueness that can be produced by being untidy. The first of the three, a tall, bald, bearded maypole of a man, was a familiar figure in the Quad in cap and gown; the gown slipped off one of his sloping shoulders. The second was very square-shouldered, short and compact, with a rather jolly grin, commonly clad in a jacket, with his gown over his arm. The third was even shorter and much shabbier, in black clerical clothes. But they all seemed suitable to Mandeville College; and the indescribable atmosphere of the two ancient and unique Universities of England. They fitted into it and they faded into it; which is there regarded as most fitting.

The two men seated on garden chairs by a little table were

a sort of brilliant blot on this grey-green landscape. They were clad mostly in black and yet they glittered from head to heel, from their burnished top-hats to their perfectly polished boots. It was dimly felt as an outrage that anybody should be so well-dressed in the well-bred freedom of Mandeville College. The only excuse was that they were foreigners. One was an American, a millionaire named Hake, dressed in the spotlessly and sparklingly gentlemanly manner known only to the rich of New York. The other, who added to all these things the outrage of an astrakhan overcoat (to say nothing of a pair of florid whiskers), was a German Count of great wealth, the shortest part of whose name was Von Zimmern. The mystery of this story, however, is not the mystery of why they were there. They were there for the reason that commonly explains the meeting of incongruous things; they proposed to give the College some money. They had come in support of a plan supported by several financiers and magnates of many countries, for founding a new Chair of Economics at Mandeville College. They had inspected the College with that tireless conscientious sightseeing of which no sons of Eve are capable except the American and the German. And now they were resting from their labours and looking solemnly at the College gardens. So far so good.

The three other men, who had already met them, passed with a vague salutation; but one of them stopped, the smallest of the three, in the black clerical clothes.

'I say,' he said, with rather the air of a frightened rabbit, 'I don't like the look of those men.'

'Good God! Who could?' ejaculated the tall man, who happened to be the Master of Mandeville. 'At least we have some rich men who don't go about dressed up like tailors' dummies.'

'Yes,' hissed the little cleric, 'that's what I mean. Like tailors' dummies.'

'Why, what do you mean?' asked the shorter of the other men, sharply.

'I mean they're like horrible waxworks,' said the cleric in a faint voice. 'I mean they don't move. Why don't they move?'

Suddenly starting out of his dim retirement, he darted across the garden and touched the German Baron on the elbow.

101

The German Baron fell over, chair and all, and the trousered legs that stuck up in the air were as stiff as the legs of the chair.

Mr Gideon P. Hake continued to gaze at the College gardens with glassy eyes; but the parallel of a waxwork confirmed the impression that they were like eyes made of glass. Somehow the rich sunlight and the coloured garden increased the creepy impression of a stiffly dressed doll; a marionette on an Italian stage. The small man in black, who was a priest named Brown, tentatively touched the millionaire on the shoulder, and the millionaire fell sideways, but horribly all of a piece, like something carved in wood.

'*Rigor mortis*,' said Father Brown, 'and so soon. But it does vary a good deal.'

The reason the first three men had joined the other two men so late (not to say too late) will best be understood by noting what had happened just inside the building, behind the Tudor archway, but a short time before they came out. They had all dined together in Hall, at the High Table; but the two foreign philanthropists, slaves of duty in the matter of seeing everything, had solemnly gone back to the chapel, of which one cloister and a staircase remained unexamined; promising to rejoin the rest in the garden, to examine as earnestly the College cigars. The rest, in a more reverent and right-minded spirit, had adjourned as usual to the long narrow oak table, round which the after-dinner wine had circulated, for all anybody knew, ever since the College had been founded in the Middle Ages by Sir John Mandeville, for the encouragement of telling stories. The Master, with the big fair beard and the bald brow, took the head of the table, and the squat man in the square jacket sat on his left; for he was the Bursar or business man of the College. Next to him, on that side of the table, sat a queer-looking man with what could only be called a crooked face; for its dark tufts of moustache and eyebrow, slanting at contrary angles, made a sort of zig-zag, as if half his face were puckered or paralysed. His name was Byles; he was the lecturer in Roman History, and his political opinions were founded on those of Coriolanus, not to mention Tarquinius Superbus. This tart Toryism, and rabidly reactionary view of all current problems, was not altogether unknown among the more old-fashioned sort of dons; but in the case of Byles there was a suggestion that it was a result rather than a cause of his acerbity. More than one sharp observer had received the impression that there was something really wrong with Byles; that some secret or some great misfortune had embittered him; as if that half-withered face had really been blasted like a storm-stricken tree. Beyond him again sat Father Brown and at the end of the table a Professor of Chemistry, large and blond and bland, with eyes that were sleepy and perhaps a little sly. It was well known that this natural philosopher regarded the other philosophers, of a more classical tradition, very much as old fogies. On the other side of the table, opposite Father Brown, was a very swarthy and silent young man, with a black pointed beard, introduced because somebody had insisted on having a Chair of Persian; opposite the sinister Byles was a very mild-looking little Chaplain, with a head like an egg. Opposite the Bursar, and at the right hand of the Master, was an empty chair; and there were many there who were glad to see it empty.

'I don't know whether Craken is coming,' said the Master, not without a nervous glance at the chair, which contrasted with the usual languid freedom of his demeanour. 'I believe in giving people a lot of rope myself; but I confess I've reached the point of being glad when he is here, merely because he isn't anywhere else.'

'Never know what he'll be up to next,' said the Bursar cheerfully, 'especially when he's instructing the young.'

'A brilliant fellow, but fiery of course,' said the Master, with a rather abrupt relapse into reserve.

'Fireworks are fiery, and also brilliant,' growled old Byles, 'but I don't want to be burned in my bed so that Craken can figure as a real Guy Fawkes.'

'Do you really *think* he would join a physical force revolution, if there were one,' asked the Bursar smiling.

'Well, *he* thinks he would,' said Byles sharply. 'Told a whole hall full of undergraduates the other day that nothing now could avert the Class War turning into a real war, with killing in the streets of the town; and it didn't matter, so long as it ended in Communism and the victory of the working-class.'

103

'The Class War,' mused the Master, with a sort of distaste mellowed by distance; for he had known William Morris long ago and been familiar enough with the more artistic and leisurely Socialists. 'I never can understand all this about the Class War. When I was young, Socialism was supposed to mean saying that there are no classes.'

''Nother way of saying that Socialists are no class,' said Byles with sour relish.

'Of course, you'd be more against them than I should,' said the Master thoughtfully, 'but I suppose my Socialism is almost as old-fashioned as your Toryism. Wonder what our young friends really think. What do you think, Baker?' he said abruptly to the Bursar on his left.

'Oh, I *don't* think, as the vulgar saying is,' said the Bursar laughing. 'You must remember I'm a very vulgar person. I'm not a thinker. I'm only a business man; and as a business man I think it's all bosh. You can't make men equal and it's damned bad business to pay them equal; especially a lot of them not worth paying for at all. Whatever it is, you've got to take the practical way out, because it's the only way out. It's not our fault if nature made everything a scramble.'

'I agree with you there,' said the Professor of Chemistry, speaking with a lisp that seemed childish in so large a man. 'Communism pretends to be oh so modern; but it is not. Throwback to the superstitions of monks and primitive tribes. A scientific government, with a really ethical responsibility to posterity, would be always looking for the line of promise and progress; not levelling and flattening it all back into the mud again. Socialism is sentimentalism; and more dangerous than a pestilence, for in that at least the fittest would survive.'

The Master smiled a little sadly. 'You know you and I will never feel quite the same about differences of opinion. Didn't somebody say up here, about walking with a friend by the river, "Not differing much, except in opinion." Isn't that the motto of a university? To have hundreds of opinions and not be opinionated. If people fall here, it's by what they are, not what they think. Perhaps I'm a relic of the eighteenth century; but I incline to the old sentimental heresy, "For forms of faith let graceless zealots fight; he can't be wrong whose life is in the right." What do you think about that, Father Brown?'

He glanced a little mischievously across at the priest and was mildly startled. For he had always found the priest very cheerful and amiable and easy to get on with; and his round face was mostly solid with good humour. But for some reason the priest's face at this moment was knotted with a frown much more sombre than any the company had ever seen on it; so that for an instant that commonplace countenance actually looked darker and more ominous than the haggard face of Byles. An instant later the cloud seemed to have passed; but Father Brown still spoke with a certain sobriety and firmness.

'I don't believe in that, anyhow,' he said shortly, 'How can his life be in the right, if his whole view of life is wrong? That's a modern muddle that arose because people didn't know how much views of life can differ. Baptists and Methodists knew they didn't differ very much in morality; but then they didn't differ very much in religion or philosophy. It's quite different when you pass from the Baptists to the Anabaptists; or from the Theosophists to the Thugs. Heresy always does affect morality, if it's heretical enough. I suppose a man may honestly believe that thieving isn't wrong. But what's the good of saying that he honestly believes in dishonesty?'

'Damned good,' said Byles with a ferocious contortion of feature, believed by many to be meant for a friendly smile. 'And that's why I object to having a Chair of Theoretical Thieving in this College.'

'Well, you're all very down on Communism, of course,' said the Master, with a sigh. 'But do you really think there's so much of it to be down on? Are any of your heresies really big enough to be dangerous?'

'I think they have grown so big,' said Father Brown gravely, 'that in some circles they are already taken for granted. They are actually unconscious. That is, without conscience.'

'And the end of it,' said Byles, 'will be the ruin of this country.'

'The end will be something worse,' said Father Brown.

A shadow shot or slid rapidly along the panelled wall opposite, as swiftly followed by the figure that had flung it; a tall but stooping figure with a vague outline like a bird of prey; accentuated by the fact that its sudden appearance and swift passage were like those of a bird startled and flying from a bush. It was only the figure of a long-limbed, high-shouldered man with long drooping moustaches, in fact, familiar enough to them all; but something in the twilight and candlelight and the flying and streaking shadow connected it strangely with the priest's unconscious words of omen; for all the world, as if those words had indeed been an augury, in the old Roman sense; and the sign of it the flight of a bird. Perhaps Mr Byles might have given a lecture on such Roman augury; and especially on that bird of ill-omen.

The tall man shot along the wall like his own shadow until he sank into the empty chair on the Master's right, and looked across at the Bursar and the rest with hollow and cavernous eyes. His hanging hair and moustache were quite fair, but his eyes were so deep-set that they might have been black. Everyone knew, or could guess, who the newcomer was; but an incident instantly followed that sufficiently illuminated the situation. The Professor of Roman History rose stiffly to his feet and stalked out of the room, indicating with little *finesse* his feelings about sitting at the same table with the Professor of Theoretical Thieving, otherwise the Communist, Mr Craken.

The Master of Mandeville covered the awkward situation with nervous grace. 'I was defending you, or some aspects of you, my dear Craken,' he said smiling, 'though I am sure you would find me quite indefensible. After all, I can't forget that the old Socialist friends of my youth had a very fine ideal of fraternity and comradeship. William Morris put it all in a sentence, "Fellowship is heaven; and lack of fellowship is hell."'

'Dons as Democrats; see headline,' said Mr Craken rather disagreeably. 'And is Hard-Case Hake going to dedicate the new Commercial Chair to the memory of William Morris?'

'Well,' said the Master, still maintaining a desperate geniality, 'I hope we may say, in a sense, that all our Chairs are Chairs of good-fellowship.'

'Yes; that's the academic version of the Morris maxim,' growled Craken. '"A Fellowship is heaven; and lack of a Fellowship is hell."'

'Don't be so cross, Craken,' interposed the Bursar briskly. 'Take some port. Tenby, pass the port to Mr Craken.'

'Oh well, I'll have a glass,' said the Communist Professor a little less ungraciously. 'I really came down here to have a smoke in the garden. Then I looked out of the window and saw your two precious millionaires were actually blooming in the garden; fresh, innocent buds. After all, it might be worth while to give them a bit of my mind.'

The Master had risen under cover of his last conventional cordiality, and was only too glad to leave the Bursar to do his best with the Wild Man. Others had risen, and the groups at the table had begun to break up; and the Bursar and Mr Craken were left more or less alone at the end of the long table. Only Father Brown continued to sit staring into vacancy with a rather cloudy expression.

'Oh, as to that,' said the Bursar. 'I'm pretty tired of them myself, to tell the truth; I've been with them the best part of a day going into facts and figures and all the business of this new Professorship. But look here, Craken,' and he leaned across the table and spoke with a sort of soft emphasis, 'you really needn't cut up so rough about this new Professorship. It doesn't really interfere with your subject. You're the only Professor of Political Economy at Mandeville and, though I don't pretend to agree with your notions, everybody knows you've got a European reputation. This is a special subject they call Applied Economics. Well, even today, as I told you, I've had a hell of a lot of Applied Economics. In other words, I've had to talk business with two business men. Would you particularly want to do that? Would you envy it? Would you stand it? Isn't that evidence enough that there is a separate subject and may well be a separate Chair?'

'Good God,' cried Craken with the intense invocation of the atheist. 'Do you think I don't want to apply Economics? Only, when we apply it, you call it red ruin and anarchy; and when you apply it, I take the liberty of calling it exploitation. If only you fellows would apply Economics, it's just possible that people might get something to eat. We are the practical people; and that's why you're afraid of us. That's why you have to get two greasy Capitalists to start another Lectureship; just because I've let the cat out of the bag.'

'Rather a wild cat, wasn't it,' said the Bursar smiling, 'that you let out of the bag?'

'And rather a gold-bag, wasn't it,' said Craken, 'that you are tying the cat up in again?'

'Well, I don't suppose we shall ever agree about all that,' said the other. 'But those fellows have come out of their chapel into the garden; and if you want to have your smoke there, you'd better come.' He watched with some amusement his companion fumbling in all his pockets till he produced a pipe, and then, gazing at it with an abstracted air, Craken rose to his feet, but even in doing so, seemed to be feeling all over himself again. Mr Baker the Bursar ended the controversy with a happy laugh of reconciliation. 'You are the practical people, and you will blow up the town with dynamite. Only you'll probably forget the dynamite, as I bet you've forgotten the tobacco. Never mind, take a fill of mine. Matches?' He threw a tobacco-pouch and its accessories across the table; to be caught by Mr Craken with that dexterity never forgotten by a cricketer, even when he adopts opinions generally regarded as not cricket. The two men rose together; but Baker could not forbear remarking, 'Are you really the only practical people? Isn't there anything to be said for the Applied Economics, that remembers to carry a tobacco-pouch as well as a pipe?'

Craken looked at him with smouldering eyes; and said at last, after slowly draining the last of his wine:

'Let's say there's another sort of practicality. I dare say I do forget details and so on. What I want you to understand is this' – he automatically returned the pouch; but his eyes were far away and jet-burning, almost terrible – 'because the inside of our intellect has changed, because we really have a new idea of right, we shall do things you think really wrong. And they will be very practical.'

'Yes,' said Father Brown, suddenly coming out of his trance. 'That's exactly what I said.'

He looked across at Craken with a glassy and rather ghastly smile, saying: 'Mr Craken and I are in complete agreement.'

'Well,' said Baker, 'Craken is going out to smoke a pipe with the plutocrats; but I doubt whether it will be a pipe of peace.'

He turned rather abruptly and called to an aged attendant in the background. Mandeville was one of the last of the very old-fashioned Colleges; and even Craken was one of the first of the Communists; before the Bolshevism of today. 'That reminds me,' the Bursar was saying, 'as you won't hand round your peace pipe, we must send out the cigars to our distinguished guests. If they're smokers they must be longing for a smoke; for they've been nosing about in the chapel since feeding-time.'

Craken exploded with a savage and jarring laugh. 'Oh, I'll take them their cigars,' he said. 'I'm only a proletarian.'

Baker and Brown and the attendant were all witnesses to the fact that the Communist strode furiously into the garden to confront the millionaires; but nothing more was seen or heard of them until, as is already recorded, Father Brown found them dead in their chairs.

It was agreed that the Master and the priest should remain to guard the scene of tragedy, while the Bursar, younger and more rapid in his movements, ran off to fetch doctors and policemen. Father Brown approached the table on which one of the cigars had burned itself away all but an inch or two; the other had dropped from the hand and been dashed out into dying sparks on the crazy-pavement. The Master of Mandeville sat down rather shakily on a sufficiently distant seat and buried his bald brow in his hands. Then he looked up at first rather wearily; and then he looked very startled indeed and broke the stillness of the garden with a word like a small explosion of horror.

There was a certain quality about Father Brown which might sometimes be called blood-curdling. He always thought about what he was doing and never about whether it was done; he would do the most ugly or horrible or undignified or dirty things as calmly as a surgeon. There was a certain blank, in his simple mind, of all those things commonly associated with being super-stitious or sentimental. He sat down on the chair from which

109

the corpse had fallen, picked up the cigar the corpse had partially smoked, carefully detached the ash, examined the butt-end and then stuck it in his mouth and lit it. It looked like some obscene and grotesque antic in derision of the dead; and it seemed to him to be the most ordinary common sense. A cloud floated upwards like the smoke of some savage sacrifice and idolatry; but to Father Brown it appeared a perfectly self-evident fact that the only way to find out what a cigar is like is to smoke it. Nor did it lessen the horror for his old friend, the Master of Mandeville, to have a dim but shrewd guess that Father Brown was, upon the possibilities of the case, risking his own life.

'No; I think that's all right,' said the priest, putting the stump down again. 'Jolly good cigars. Your cigars. Not American or German. I don't think there's anything odd about the cigar itself; but they'd better take care of the ashes. These men were poisoned somehow with the sort of stuff that stiffens the body quickly . . . By the way, there goes somebody who knows more about it than we do.'

The Master sat up with a curiously uncomfortable jolt; for indeed the large shadow which had fallen across the pathway preceded a figure which, however heavy, was almost as soft-footed as a shadow. Professor Wadham, eminent occupant of the Chair of Chemistry, always moved very quietly in spite of his size, and there was nothing odd about his strolling in the garden; yet there seemed something unnaturally neat in his appearing at the exact moment when chemistry was mentioned.

Professor Wadham prided himself on his quietude; some would say his insensibility. He did not turn a hair on his flattened flaxen head, but stood looking down at the dead men with a shade of something like indifference on his large froglike face. Only when he looked at the cigar-ash, which the priest had preserved, he touched it with one finger; then he seemed to stand even stiller than before; but in the shadow of his face his eyes for an instant seemed to shoot out telescopically like one of his own microscopes. He had certainly realized or recognized something; but he said nothing.

'I don't know where anyone is to begin in this business,' said the Master.

'I should begin,' said Father Brown, 'by asking where these unfortunate men had been most of the time today.'

'They were messing about in my laboratory for a good time,' said Wadham, speaking for the first time. 'Baker often comes up to have a chat, and this time he brought his two patrons to inspect my department. But I think they went everywhere; real tourists. I know they went to the chapel and even into the tunnel under the crypt, where you have to light candles; instead of digesting their food like sane men. Baker seems to have taken them everywhere.'

'Were they interested in anything particular in your department?' asked the priest. 'What were you doing there just then?'

The Professor of Chemistry murmured a chemical formula beginning with 'sulphate', and ending with something that sounded like 'silenium'; unintelligible to both his hearers. He then wandered wearily away and sat on a remote bench in the sun, closing his eyes, but turning up his large face with heavy forbearance.

At this point, by a sharp contrast, the lawns were crossed by a brisk figure travelling as rapidly and as straight as a bullet; and Father Brown recognized the neat black clothes and shrewd doglike face of a police-surgeon whom he had met in the poorer parts of the town. He was the first to arrive of the official contingent.

'Look here,' said the Master to the priest, before the doctor was within earshot, 'I must know something. Did you mean what you said about Communism being a real danger and leading to crime?'

'Yes,' said Father Brown smiling rather grimly, 'I have really noticed the spread of some Communist ways and influences; and, in one sense, this is a Communist crime.'

'Thank you,' said the Master. 'Then I must go off and see to something at once. Tell the authorities I'll be back in ten minutes.'

The Master had vanished into one of the Tudor archways at just about the moment when the police-doctor had reached the table and cheerfully recognized Father Brown. On the latter's suggestion that they should sit down at the tragic table, Dr Blake threw one sharp and doubtful glance at the big, bland and seemingly somnolent chemist, who occupied a more remote seat. He was duly informed of the Professor's identity, and what had so far been gathered of the Professor's evidence; and listened to it silently while conducting a preliminary examination of the dead bodies. Naturally, he seemed more concentrated on the actual corpses than on the hearsay evidence, until one detail suddenly distracted him entirely from the science of anatomy.

'What did the Professor say he was working at?' he inquired.

Father Brown patiently repeated the chemical formula he did not understand.

'*What*?' snapped Dr Blake, like a pistol-shot. 'Gosh! This is pretty frightful!'

'Because it's poison?' inquired Father Brown.

'Because it's piffle,' replied Dr Blake. 'It's simply nonsense. The Professor is quite a famous chemist. Why is a famous chemist deliberately talking nonsense?'

'Well, I think I know that one,' answered Father Brown mildly. 'He is talking nonsense, because he is telling lies. He is concealing something; and he wanted specially to conceal it from these two men and their representatives.'

The doctor lifted his eyes from the two men and looked across at the almost unnaturally immobile figure of the great chemist. He might almost have been asleep; a garden butterfly had settled upon him and seemed to turn his stillness into that of a stone idol. The large folds of his froglike face reminded the doctor of the hanging skins of a rhinoceros.

'Yes,' said Father Brown, in a very low voice. 'He is a wicked man.'

'God damn it all!' cried the doctor, suddenly moved to his very depths. 'Do you mean that a great scientific man like that deals in murder?'

'Fastidious critics would have complained of his dealing in murder,' said the priest dispassionately. 'I don't say I'm very fond of people dealing in murder in that way myself. But what's much more to the point – I'm sure that *these* poor fellows were among his fastidious critics.'

'You mean they found his secret and he silenced them?' said Blake frowning. 'But what in hell was his secret? How could a man murder on a large scale in a place like this?'

'I have told you his secret,' said the priest. 'It is a secret of the soul. He is a bad man. For heaven's sake don't fancy I say that because he and I are of opposite schools or traditions. I have a crowd of scientific friends; and most of them are heroically disinterested. Even of the most sceptical, I would only say they are rather irrationally disinterested. But now and then you do get a man who is a materialist, in the sense of a beast. I repeat he's a bad man. Much worse than –' And Father Brown seemed to hesitate for a word.

'You mean much worse than the Communist?' suggested the other.

'No; I mean much worse than the murderer,' said Father Brown.

He got to his feet in an abstracted manner; and hardly realized that his companion was staring at him.

'But didn't you mean,' asked Blake at last, 'that this Wadham is the murderer?'

'Oh, no,' said Father Brown more cheerfully. 'The murderer is a much more sympathetic and understandable person. He at least was desperate; and had the excuses of sudden rage and despair.'

'Why,' cried the doctor, 'do you mean it was the Communist after all?'

It was at this very moment, appropriately enough, that the police officials appeared with an announcement that seemed to conclude the case in a most decisive and satisfactory manner. They had been somewhat delayed in reaching the scene of the crime, by the simple fact that they had already captured the criminal. Indeed, they had captured him almost at the gates of their own official residence. They had already had reason to suspect the activities of Craken the Communist during various disorders in the town; when they heard of the outrage they felt it safe to arrest him; and found the arrest thoroughly justified. For, as Inspector Cook radiantly explained to dons and doctors on the lawn of Mandeville garden, no sooner was the notorious

THE SCANDAL OF FATHER BROWN

Communist searched, than it was found that he was actually carrying a box of poisoned matches.

The moment Father Brown heard the word 'matches', he jumped from his seat as if a match had been lighted under him.

'Ah,' he cried, with a sort of universal radiance, 'and now it's all clear.'

'What do you mean by all clear?' demanded the Master of Mandeville, who had returned in all the pomp of his own officialism to match the pomp of the police officials now occupying the College like a victorious army. 'Do you mean you are convinced now that the case against Craken is clear?'

'I mean that Craken is cleared,' said Father Brown firmly, 'and the case against Craken is cleared away. Do you really believe Craken is the kind of man who would go about poisoning people with matches?'

'That's all very well,' replied the Master, with the troubled expression he had never lost since the first sensation occurred. 'But it was you yourself who said that fanatics with false principles may do wicked things. For that matter, it was you yourself who said that Communism is cropping up everywhere and Communistic habits spreading.'

Father Brown laughed in a rather shamefaced manner.

'As to the last point,' he said, 'I suppose I owe you all an apology. I seem to be always making a mess of things with my silly little jokes.'

'Jokes!' repeated the Master, staring rather indignantly.

'Well,' explained the priest, rubbing his head. 'When I talked about a Communist habit spreading, I only meant a habit I happen to have noticed about two or three times even today. It is a Communist habit by no means confined to Communists. It is the extraordinary habit of so many men, especially Englishmen, of putting other people's matchboxes in their pockets without remembering to return them. Of course, it seems an awfully silly little trifle to talk about. But it does happen to be the way the crime was committed.'

'It sounds to me quite crazy,' said the doctor.

'Well, if almost any man may forget to return matches, you

can bet your boots that Craken would forget to return them. So the poisoner who had prepared the matches got rid of them on to Craken, by the simple process of lending them and not getting them back. A really admirable way of shedding responsibility; because Craken himself would be perfectly unable to imagine where he had got them from. But when he used them quite innocently to light the cigars he offered to our two visitors, he was caught in an obvious trap; one of those too obvious traps. He was the bold bad Revolutionist murdering two millionaires.'

'Well, who else would want to murder them?' growled the doctor.

'Ah, who indeed?' replied the priest; and his voice changed to much greater gravity. 'There we come to the other thing I told you; and that, let me tell you, was not a joke. I told you that heresies and false doctrines had become common and conversational; that everybody was used to them; that nobody really noticed them. Did you think I meant *Communism* when I said that? Why, it was just the other way. You were all as nervous as cats about Communism; and you watched Craken like a wolf. Of course, Communism is a heresy; but it isn't a heresy that you people take for granted. It is Capitalism you take for granted; or rather the vices of Capitalism disguised as a dead Darwinism. Do you recall what you were all saying in the Common Room, about life being only a scramble, and nature demanding the survival of the fittest, and how it doesn't matter whether the poor are paid justly or not? Why, *that* is the heresy that you have grown accustomed to, my friends; and it's every bit as much a heresy as Communism. That's the anti-Christian morality or immorality that you take quite naturally. And that's the immorality that has made a man a murderer today.'

'What man?' cried the Master, and his voice cracked with a sudden weakness.

'Let me approach it another way,' said the priest placidly. 'You all talk as if Craken ran away; but he didn't. When the two men toppled over, he ran down the street, summoned the doctor merely by shouting through the window, and shortly afterwards was trying to summon the police. That was how he was arrested. But doesn't it strike you, now one comes to think of it, that Mr Baker the Bursar is rather a long time looking for the police?'

'What is he doing then?' asked the Master sharply.

'I fancy he's destroying papers; or perhaps ransacking these men's rooms to see they haven't left us a letter. Or it may have something to do with our friend Wadham. Where does he come in? That is really very simple and a sort of joke too. Mr Wadham is experimenting in poisons for the next war; and has something of which a whiff of flame will stiffen a man dead. Of course, he had nothing to do with killing these men; but he did conceal his chemical secret for a very simple reason. One of them was a Puritan Yankee and the other a cosmopolitan Jew; and those two types are often fanatical Pacifists. They would have called it planning murder and probably refused to help the College. But Baker was a friend of Wadham and it was easy for him to dip matches in the new material.'

Another peculiarity of the little priest was that his mind was all of a piece, and he was unconscious of many incongruities; he would change the note of his talk from something quite public to something quite private, without any particular embarrassment. On this occasion, he made most of the company stare with mystification, by beginning to talk to one person when he had just been talking to ten; quite indifferent to the fact that only the one could have any notion of what he was talking about.

'I'm sorry if I misled you, doctor, by that maundering metaphysical digression on the man of sin,' he said apologetically. 'Of course it had nothing to do with the murder; but the truth is I'd forgotten all about the murder for the moment. I'd forgotten everything, you see, but a sort of vision of that fellow, with his vast unhuman face, squatting among the flowers like some blind monster of the Stone Age. And I was thinking that some men are pretty monstrous, like men of stone; but it was all irrelevant. Being bad inside has very little to do with committing crimes outside. The worst criminals have committed no crimes. The practical point is why did the practical criminal commit this crime. Why did Baker the Bursar want to kill these men? That's all that concerns us now. The answer is the answer to the question I've asked twice. Where were these men most of the time, apart from nosing in chapels or laboratories? By the Bursar's own account, they were talking business with the Bursar.

'Now, with all respect to the dead, I do not exactly grovel before the intellect of these two financiers. Their views on economics and ethics were heathen and heartless. Their views on Peace were tosh. Their views on Port were even more deplorable. But one thing they did understand; and that was business. And it took them a remarkably short time to discover that the business man in charge of the funds of this College was a swindler. Or shall I say, a true follower of the doctrine of the unlimited struggle for life and the survival of the fittest.'

'You mean they were going to expose him and he killed them before they could speak,' said the doctor frowning. 'There are a lot of details I don't understand.'

'There are some details I'm not sure of myself,' said the priest frankly. 'I suspect all that business of candles underground had something to do with abstracting the millionaires' own matches, or perhaps making sure they had no matches. But I'm sure of the main gesture, the gay and careless gesture of Baker tossing his matches to the careless Craken. That gesture was the murderous blow.'

'There's one thing I don't understand,' said the Inspector. 'How did Baker know that Craken wouldn't light up himself then and there at the table and become an unwanted corpse?'

The face of Father Brown became almost heavy with reproach; and his voice had a sort of mournful yet generous warmth in it.

'Well, hang it all,' he said, 'he was only an atheist.'

'I'm afraid I don't know what you mean,' said the Inspector, politely.

'He only wanted to abolish God,' explained Father Brown in a temperate and reasonable tone. 'He only wanted to destroy the Ten Commandments and root up all the religion and civilization that had made him, and wash out all the common sense of ownership and honesty; and let his culture and his country be flattened out by savages from the ends of the earth. That's all he wanted. You have no right to accuse him of anything beyond that. Hang it all, everybody draws the line somewhere! And you come here and calmly suggest that a Mandeville Man of the old generation (for Craken was of the old generation, whatever his views) would have begun to smoke, or even strike a match, while he was still drinking the College Port, of the vintage of '08 – no, no; men are not so utterly without laws and limits as all that! I was there; I saw him; he had not finished his wine, and you ask me why he did not *smoke*! No such anarchic question has ever shaken the arches of Mandeville College ... Funny place, Mandeville College. Funny place, Oxford. Funny place, England.'

'But you haven't anything particular to do with Oxford?' asked the doctor curiously.

'I have to do with England,' said Father Brown. 'I come from there. And the funniest thing of all is that even if you love it and belong to it, you still can't make head or tail of it.'

SEVEN

The Point of a Pin

FATHER BROWN always declared that he solved this problem in his sleep. And this was true, though in rather an odd fashion; because it occurred at a time when his sleep was rather disturbed. It was disturbed very early in the morning by the hammering that began in the huge building, or half-building, that was in process of erection opposite to his rooms; a colossal pile of flats still mostly covered with scaffolding and with boards announcing Messrs Swindon & Sand as the builders and owners. The hammering was renewed at regular intervals and was easily recognizable: because Messrs Swindon & Sand specialized in some new American system of cement flooring which, in spite of its subsequent smoothness, solidity, impenetrability and permanent comfort (as described in the advertisements), had to be clamped down at certain points with heavy tools. Father Brown endeavoured, however, to extract exiguous comfort from it; saying that it always woke him up in time for the very earliest Mass, and was therefore something almost in the nature of a carillon. After all, he said, it was almost as poetic that Christians should be awakened by hammers as by bells. As a fact, however, the building operations were a little on his nerves, for another reason. For there was hanging like a cloud over the half-built skyscraper the possibility of a Labour crisis, which the newspapers doggedly insisted on describing as a Strike. As a matter of fact, if ever it happened, it would be a Lock-out. But he worried a good deal about whether it would happen. And it might be questioned whether hammering is more of a strain on the attention because it may go on for ever, or because it may stop at any minute.

'As a mere matter of taste and fancy,' said Father Brown, staring up at the edifice with his owlish spectacles, 'I rather wish it would stop. I wish all houses would stop while they still have the scaffolding up. It seems almost a pity that houses are ever finished. They look so fresh and hopeful with all that fairy filigree of white wood, all light and bright in the sun; and a man so often only finishes a house by turning it into a tomb.'

As he turned away from the object of his scrutiny, he nearly ran into a man who had just darted across the road towards him. It was a man whom he knew slightly, but sufficiently to regard him (in the circumstances) as something of a bird of ill-omen. Mr Mastyk was a squat man with a square head that looked hardly European, dressed with a heavy dandyism that seemed rather too consciously Europeanized. But Brown had seen him lately talking to young Sand of the building firm; and he did not like it. This man Mastyk was the head of an organization rather new in English industrial politics; produced by extremes at both ends; a definite army of non-Union and largely alien labour hired out in gangs to various firms; and he was obviously hovering about in the hope of hiring it out to this one. In short, he might negotiate some way of out-manoeuvring the Trade Union and flooding the works with blacklegs. Father Brown had been drawn into some of the debates, being in some sense called in on both sides. And as the Capitalists all reported that, to their positive knowledge, he was a Bolshevist; and as the Bolshevists all testified that he was a reactionary rigidly attached to *bourgeois* ideologies, it may be inferred that he talked a certain amount of sense without any appreciable effect on anybody. The news brought by Mr Mastyk, however, was calculated to jerk everybody out of the ordinary rut of the dispute.

'They want you to go over there at once,' said Mr Mastyk, in awkwardly accented English. 'There is a threat to murder.'

Father Brown followed his guide in silence up several stairways and ladders to a platform of the unfinished building, on which were grouped the more or less familiar figures of the heads of the building business. They included even what had once been the head of it; though the head had been for some time rather a head in the clouds. It was at least a head in a coronet, that hid it from human sight like a cloud. Lord Stanes, in other words, had not only retired from the business but been caught up into the House of Lords and disappeared. His rare reappearances were languid and somewhat dreary; but this one, in conjunction with that of Mastyk, seemed none the less menacing. Lord Stanes was a lean, long-headed, hollow-eyed man with very faint fair hair fading into baldness; and he was the most evasive person the priest had ever met. He was unrivalled in the true Oxford talent of saying, 'No doubt you're right,' so as to sound like, 'No doubt you think you're right,' or of merely remarking, 'You think so?' so as to imply the acid addition, 'You would.' But Father Brown fancied that the man was not merely bored but faintly embittered, though whether at being called down from Olympus to control such trade squabbles, or merely at not being really any longer in control of them, it was difficult to guess.

On the whole, Father Brown rather preferred the more *bourgeois* group of partners, Sir Hubert Sand and his nephew Henry; though he doubted privately whether they really had very many ideologies. True, Sir Hubert Sand had obtained considerable celebrity in the newspapers; both as a patron of sport and as a patriot in many crises during and after the Great War. He had won notable distinction in France, for a man of his years, and had afterwards been featured as a triumphant captain of industry overcoming difficulties among the munition-workers. He had been called a Strong Man; but that was not his fault. He was in fact a heavy, hearty Englishman; a great swimmer; a good squire; an admirable amateur colonel. Indeed, something that can only be called a military make-up pervaded his appearance. He was growing stout, but he kept his shoulders set back; his curly hair and moustache were still brown while the colours of his face were already somewhat withered and faded. His nephew was a burly youth of the pushing, or rather shouldering, sort with a relatively small head thrust out on a thick neck, as if he went at things with his head down; a gesture somehow rendered rather quaint and boyish by the pince-nez that were balanced on his pugnacious pug-nose.

Father Brown had looked at all these things before; and at that moment everybody was looking at something entirely new.

In the centre of the wood-work there was nailed up a large loose flapping piece of paper on which something was scrawled in crude and almost crazy capital letters, as if the writer were either almost illiterate or were affecting or parodying illiteracy. The words actually ran: 'The Council of the Workers warns Hubert Sand that he will lower wages and lock out workmen at his peril. If the notices go out tomorrow, he will be dead by the justice of the people.'

Lord Stanes was just stepping back from his examination of the paper, and, looking across at his partner, he said with rather a curious intonation:

'Well, it's you they want to murder. Evidently I'm not considered worth murdering.'

One of those still electric shocks of fancy that sometimes thrilled Father Brown's mind in an almost meaningless way shot through him at that particular instant. He had a queer notion that the man who was speaking could not now be murdered, because he was already dead. It was, he cheerfully admitted, a perfectly senseless idea. But there was something that always gave him the creeps about the cold disenchanted detachment of the noble senior partner; about his cadaverous colour and inhospitable eyes. 'The fellow,' he thought in the same perverse mood, 'has green eyes and looks as if he had green blood.'

Anyhow, it was certain that Sir Hubert Sand had not got green blood. His blood, which was red enough in every sense, was creeping up into his withered or weather-beaten cheeks with all the warm fullness of life that belongs to the natural and innocent indignation of the good-natured.

'In all my life,' he said, in a strong voice and yet shakily, 'I have never had such a thing said or done about me. I may have differed –'

'We can none of us differ about this,' struck in his nephew impetuously. 'I've tried to get on with them, but this is a bit too thick.'

'You don't really think,' began Father Brown, 'that your workmen –'

'I say we may have differed,' said old Sand, still a little

tremulously, 'God knows I never liked the idea of threatening English workmen with cheaper labour –'

'We none of us liked it,' said the young man, 'but if I know you, uncle, this has about settled it.'

Then after a pause he added, 'I suppose, as you say, we did disagree about details; but as to real policy –'

'My dear fellow,' said his uncle, comfortably. 'I hoped there would never be any real disagreement.' From which anybody who understands the English nation may rightly infer that there had been very considerable disagreement. Indeed the uncle and nephew differed almost as much as an Englishman and an American. The uncle had the English ideal of getting outside the business, and setting up a sort of an alibi as a country gentleman. The nephew had the American ideal of getting inside the business; of getting inside the very mechanism like a mechanic. And, indeed, he had worked with most of the mechanics and was familiar with most of the processes and tricks of the trade. And he was American again, in the fact that he did this partly as an employer to keep his men up to the mark, but in some vague way also as an equal, or at least with a pride in showing himself also as a worker. For this reason he had often appeared almost as a representative of the workers, on technical points which were a hundred miles away from his uncle's popular eminence in politics or sport. The memory of those many occasions, when young Henry had practically come out of the workshop in his shirt-sleeves, to demand some concession about the conditions of the work, lent a peculiar force and even violence to his present reaction the other way.

'Well, they've damned-well locked themselves out this time,' he cried. 'After a threat like that there's simply nothing left but to defy them. There's nothing left but to sack them all now; instanter; on the spot. Otherwise we'll be the laughing-stock of the world.'

Old Sand frowned with equal indignation, but began slowly: 'I shall be very much criticized –'

'Criticized!' cried the young man shrilly. 'Criticized if you defy a threat of murder! Have you any notion how you'll be criticized if you don't defy it? Won't you enjoy the headlines?

"Great Capitalist Terrorized" – "Employer Yields to Murder Threat."'

'Particularly,' said Lord Stanes, with something faintly unpleasant in his tone. 'Particularly when he has been in so many headlines already as "The Strong Man of Steel-Building."'

Sand had gone very red again and his voice came thickly from under his thick moustache. 'Of course you're right there. If these brutes think I'm afraid –'

At this point there was an interruption in the conversation of the group; and a slim young man came towards them swiftly. The first notable thing about him was that he was one of those whom men, and women too, think are just a little too nice-looking to look nice. He had beautiful dark curly hair and a silken moustache and he spoke like a gentleman, but with almost too refined and exactly modulated an accent. Father Brown knew him at once as Rupert Rae, the secretary of Sir Hubert, whom he had often seen pottering about in Sir Hubert's house; but never with such impatience in his movements or such a wrinkle on his brow.

'I'm sorry, sir,' he said to his employer, 'but there's a man been hanging about over there. I've done my best to get rid of him. He's only got a letter, but he swears he must give it to you personally.'

'You mean he went first to my house?' said Sand, glancing swiftly at his secretary. 'I suppose you've been there all the morning.'

'Yes, sir,' said Mr Rupert Rae.

There was a short silence; and then Sir Hubert Sand curtly intimated that the man had better be brought along; and the man duly appeared.

Nobody, not even the least fastidious lady, would have said that the newcomer was too nice-looking. He had very large ears and a face like a frog, and he stared before him with an almost ghastly fixity, which Father Brown attributed to his having a glass eye. In fact, his fancy was tempted to equip the man with two glass eyes; with so glassy a stare did he contemplate the company. But the priest's experience, as distinct from his fancy, was able to suggest several natural causes for that unnatural waxwork glare; one of them being an abuse of the divine gift of fermented liquor. The man was short and shabby and carried a large bowler hat in one hand and a large sealed letter in the other.

Sir Hubert Sand looked at him; and then said quietly enough, but in a voice that somehow seemed curiously small, coming out of the fullness of his bodily presence: 'Oh – it's you.'

He held out his hand for the letter; and then looked around apologetically, with poised finger, before ripping it open and reading it. When he had read it, he stuffed it into his inside pocket and said hastily and a little harshly:

'Well, I suppose all this business is over, as you say. No more negotiations possible now; we couldn't pay the wages they want anyhow. But I shall want to see you again, Henry, about – about winding things up generally.'

'All right,' said Henry, a little sulkily perhaps, as if he would have preferred to wind them up by himself. 'I shall be up in number 188 after lunch; got to know how far they've got up there.'

The man with the glass eye, if it was a glass eye, stumped stiffly away; and the eye of Father Brown (which was by no means a glass eye) followed him thoughtfully as he threaded his way through the ladders and disappeared into the street.

It was on the following morning that Father Brown had the unusual experience of over-sleeping himself; or at least of starting from sleep with a subjective conviction that he must be late. This was partly due to his remembering, as a man may remember a dream, the fact of having been half-awakened at a more regular hour and fallen asleep again; a common enough occurrence with most of us, but a very uncommon occurrence with Father Brown. And he was afterwards oddly convinced, with that mystic side of him which was normally turned away from the world, that in that detached dark islet of dreamland, between the two wakings, there lay like buried treasure the truth of this tale.

As it was, he jumped up with great promptitude, plunged into his clothes, seized his big knobby umbrella and bustled out into the street, where the bleak white morning was breaking like splintered ice about the huge black building facing him. He was surprised to find that the streets shone almost empty in the cold crystalline light; the very look of it told him it could hardly be so late as he had feared. Then suddenly the stillness was cloven by the arrowlike swiftness of a long grey car which halted before the big deserted flats. Lord Stanes unfolded himself from within and approached the door, carrying (rather languidly) two large suitcases. At the same moment the door opened, and somebody seemed to step back instead of stepping out into the street. Stanes called twice to the man within, before that person seemed to complete his original gesture by coming out on to the doorstep; then the two held a brief colloquy, ending in the nobleman carrying his suitcases upstairs, and the other coming out into full daylight and revealing the heavy shoulders and peering head of young Henry Sand.

Father Brown made no more of this rather odd meeting, until two days later the young man drove up in his own car, and implored the priest to enter it. 'Something awful has happened,' he said, 'and I'd rather talk to you than Stanes. You know Stanes arrived the other day with some mad idea of camping in one of the flats that's just finished. That's why I had to go there early and open the door to him. But all that will keep. I want you to come up to my uncle's place at once.'

'Is he ill?' inquired the priest quickly.

'I think he's dead,' answered the nephew.

'What do you mean by saying you think he's dead?' asked Father Brown a little briskly. 'Have you got a doctor?'

'No,' answered the other. 'I haven't got a doctor or a patient either ... It's no good calling in doctors to examine the body; because the body has run away. But I'm afraid I know where it has run to ... the truth is – we kept it dark for two days; but he's disappeared.'

'Wouldn't it be better,' said Father Brown mildly, 'if you told me what has really happened from the beginning?'

'I know,' answered Henry Sand; 'it's an infernal shame to talk flippantly like this about the poor old boy; but people get like that when they're rattled. I'm not much good at hiding things; the long and the short of it is – well, I won't tell you the long of it now. It's what some people would call rather a long shot; shooting suspicions at random and so on. But the short of it is that my unfortunate uncle has committed suicide.'

They were by this time skimming along in the car through the last fringes of the town and the first fringes of the forest and park beyond it; the lodge gates of Sir Hubert Sand's small estate were about half a mile farther on amid the thickening throng of the beeches. The estate consisted chiefly of a small park and a large ornamental garden, which descended in terraces of a certain classical pomp to the very edge of the chief river of the district. As soon as they arrived at the house, Henry took the priest somewhat hastily through the old Georgian rooms and out upon the other side; where they silently descended the slope, a rather steep slope embanked with flowers, from which they could see the pale river spread out before them almost as flat as in a bird's-eye view. They were just turning the corner of the path under an enormous classical urn crowned with a somewhat incongruous garland of geraniums, when Father Brown saw a movement in the bushes and thin trees just below him, that seemed as swift as a movement of startled birds.

In the tangle of thin trees by the river two figures seemed to divide or scatter; one of them glided swiftly into the shadows and the other came forward to face them; bringing them to a halt and an abrupt and rather unaccountable silence. Then Henry Sand said in his heavy way: 'I think you know Father Brown . . . Lady Sand.'

Father Brown did know her; but at that moment he might almost have said that he did not know her. The pallor and constriction of her face was like a mask of tragedy; she was much younger than her husband, but at that moment she looked somehow older than everything in that old house and garden. And the priest remembered, with a subconscious thrill, that she was indeed older in type and lineage and was the true possessor of the place. For her own family had owned it as impoverished aristocrats, before she had restored its fortunes by marrying a successful business man. As she stood there, she might have been a family picture, or even a family ghost. Her pale face was of that pointed yet oval type seen in some old pictures of Mary Queen of Scots; and its expression seemed almost to go beyond the natural unnaturalness of a situation, in which her husband had vanished under suspicion of suicide. Father Brown, with the same subconscious movement of the mind, wondered who it was with whom she had been talking among the trees.

'I suppose you know all this dreadful news,' she said, with a comfortless composure. 'Poor Hubert must have broken down under all this revolutionary persecution, and been just maddened into taking his own life. I don't know whether you can do anything; or whether these horrible Bolsheviks can be made responsible for hounding him to death.'

'I am terribly distressed, Lady Sand,' said Father Brown. 'And still, I must own, a little bewildered. You speak of persecution; do you think that anybody could hound him to death merely by pinning up that paper on the wall?'

'I fancy,' answered the lady, with a darkening brow, 'that there were other persecutions besides the paper.'

'It shows what mistakes one may make,' said the priest sadly. 'I never should have thought he would be so illogical as to die in order to avoid death.'

'I know,' she answered, gazing at him gravely. 'I should never have believed it, if it hadn't been written with his own hand.'

'What?' cried Father Brown, with a little jump like a rabbit that has been shot at.

'Yes,' said Lady Sand calmly. 'He left a confession of suicide; so I fear there is no doubt about it.' And she passed on up the slope alone, with all the inviolable isolation of the family ghost.

The spectacles of Father Brown were turned in mute inquiry to the eyeglasses of Mr Henry Sand. And the latter gentleman, after an instant's hesitation, spoke again in his rather blind and plunging fashion: 'Yes, you see, it seems pretty clear now what he did. He was always a great swimmer and used to come down in his dressing-gown every morning for a dip in the river. Well, he came down as usual, and left his dressing-gown on the bank; it's lying there still. But he also left a message saying he was going for his last swim and then death, or something like that.'

'Where did he leave the message?' asked Father Brown.

'He scrawled it on that tree there, overhanging the water, I suppose the last thing he took hold of; just below where the dressing-gown's lying. Come and see for yourself.'

Father Brown ran down the last short slope to the shore and peered under the hanging tree, whose plumes were almost dipping in the stream. Sure enough, he saw on the smooth bark the words scratched conspicuously and unmistakably: 'One more swim and then drowning. Good-bye. Hubert Sand.' Father Brown's gaze travelled slowly up the bank till it rested on a gorgeous rag of raiment, all red and yellow with gilded tassels. It was the dressing-gown and the priest picked it up and began to turn it over. Almost as he did so he was conscious that a figure had flashed across his field of vision; a tall dark figure that slipped from one clump of trees to another, as if following the trail of the vanishing lady. He had little doubt that it was the companion from whom she had lately parted. He had still less doubt that it was the dead man's secretary, Mr Rupert Rae.

'Of course, it might be a final after-thought to leave the message,' said Father Brown, without looking up, his eye riveted on the red and gold garment. 'We've all heard of love-messages written on trees; and I suppose there might be death-messages written on trees too.'

'Well, he wouldn't have anything in the pockets of his dressing-gown, I suppose,' said young Sand. 'And a man might naturally scratch his message on a tree if he had no pens, ink or paper.'

'Sounds like French exercises,' said the priest dismally. 'But I wasn't thinking of that.' Then, after a silence, he said in a rather altered voice:

'To tell the truth, I was thinking whether a man might not naturally scratch his message on a tree, even if he had stacks of pens, and quarts of ink, and reams of paper.'

Henry was looking at him with a rather startled air, his eyeglasses crooked on his pug-nose. 'And what do you mean by that?' he asked sharply.

'Well,' said Father Brown slowly, 'I don't exactly mean that postmen will carry letters in the form of logs, or that you will ever drop a line to a friend by putting a postage stamp on a pine-tree. It would have to be a particular sort of position – in fact, it

129

would have to be a particular sort of person, who really preferred this sort of arboreal correspondence. But, given the position and the person, I repeat what I said. He would still write on a tree, as the song says, if all the world were paper and all the sea were ink; if that river flowed with everlasting ink or all these woods were a forest of quills and fountain-pens.'

It was evident that Sand felt something creepy about the priest's fanciful imagery; whether because he found it incomprehensible or because he was beginning to comprehend.

'You see,' said Father Brown, turning the dressing-gown over slowly as he spoke, 'a man isn't expected to write his very best handwriting when he chips it on a tree. And if the man were not the man, if I make myself clear – Hullo!'

He was looking down at the red dressing-gown, and it seemed for the moment as if some of the red had come off on his finger; but both the faces turned towards it were already a shade paler.

'Blood!' said Father Brown; and for the instant there was a deadly stillness save for the melodious noises of the river.

Henry Sand cleared his throat and nose with noises that were by no means melodious. Then he said rather hoarsely: 'Whose blood?'

'Oh, mine,' said Father Brown; but he did not smile.

A moment after he said: 'There was a pin in this thing and I pricked myself. But I don't think you quite appreciate the point ... the point of the pin, I do'; and he sucked his finger like a child.

'You see,' he said after another silence, 'the gown was folded up and pinned together; nobody could have unfolded it – at least without scratching himself. In plain words, Hubert Sand never *wore* this dressing-gown. Any more than Hubert Sand ever wrote on that tree. Or drowned himself in that river.'

The pince-nez tilted on Henry's inquiring nose fell off with a click; but he was otherwise motionless, as if rigid with surprise.

'Which brings us back,' went on Father Brown cheerfully, 'to somebody's taste for writing his private correspondence on trees, like Hiawatha and his picture-writing. Sand had all the time there was, before drowning himself. Why didn't he leave a note for his wife like a sane man? Or, shall we say ... Why didn't the Other Man leave a note for the wife like a sane man? Because he would have had to forge the husband's handwriting; always a tricky thing now that experts are so nosey about it. But nobody can be expected to imitate even his own handwriting, let alone somebody else's, when he carves capital letters in the bark of a tree. This is not a suicide, Mr Sand. If it's anything at all, it's a murder.'

The bracken and bushes of the undergrowth snapped and crackled as the big young man rose out of them like a leviathan, and stood lowering, with his thick neck thrust forward.

'I'm no good at hiding things,' he said, 'and I half-suspected something like this – expected it, you might say, for a long time. To tell the truth, I could hardly be civil to the fellow – to either of them, for that matter.'

'What exactly do you mean?' asked the priest, looking him gravely full in the face.

'I mean,' said Henry Sand, 'that you have shown me the murder and I think I could show you the murderers.'

Father Brown was silent and the other went on rather jerkily.

'You said people sometimes wrote love-messages on trees. Well, as a fact, there are some of them on that tree; there are two sort of monograms twisted together up there under the leaves – I suppose you know that Lady Sand was the heiress of this place long before she married; and she knew that damned dandy of a secretary even in those days. I guess they used to meet here and write their vows upon the trysting-tree. They seem to have used the trysting-tree for another purpose later on. Sentiment, no doubt, or economy.'

'They must be very horrible people,' said Father Brown.

'Haven't there been any horrible people in history or the police-news?' demanded Sand with some excitement. 'Haven't there been lovers who made love seem more horrible than hate? Don't you know about Bothwell and all the bloody legends of such lovers?'

'I know the legend of Bothwell,' answered the priest. 'I also know it to be quite legendary. But of course it's true that husbands have been sometimes put away like that. By the way, where was he put away? I mean, where did they hide the body?'

'I suppose they drowned him, or threw him in the water when he was dead,' snorted the young man impatiently.

Father Brown blinked thoughtfully and then said: 'A river is a good place to hide an imaginary body. It's a rotten bad place to hide a real one. I mean, it's easy to *say* you've thrown it in, because it *might* be washed away to sea. But if you really did throw it in, it's about a hundred to one it wouldn't; the chances of it going ashore somewhere are enormous. I think they must have had a better scheme for hiding the body than that – or the body would have been found by now. And if there were any marks of violence –'

'Oh, bother hiding the body,' said Henry, with some irritation; 'haven't we witness enough in the writing on their own devilish tree?'

'The body is the chief witness in every murder,' answered the other. 'The hiding of the body, nine times out of ten, is the practical problem to be solved.'

There was a silence; and Father Brown continued to turn over the red dressing-gown and spread it out on the shining grass of the sunny shore; he did not look up. But, for some time past he had been conscious that the whole landscape had been changed for him by the presence of a third party; standing as still as a statue in the garden.

'By the way,' he said, lowering his voice, 'how do you explain that little guy with the glass eye, who brought your poor uncle a letter yesterday? It seemed to me he was entirely altered by reading it; that's why I wasn't surprised at the suicide, when I thought it was a suicide. That chap was a rather low-down private detective, or I'm much mistaken.'

'Why,' said Henry in a hesitating manner, 'why, he might have been – husbands do sometimes put on detectives in domestic tragedies like this, don't they? I suppose he'd got the proofs of their intrigue; and so they –'

'I shouldn't talk too loud,' said Father Brown, 'because your detective is detecting us at this moment, from about a yard beyond those bushes.'

They looked up, and sure enough the goblin with the glass eye was fixing them with that disagreeable optic, looking all the more grotesque for standing among the white and waxen blooms of the classical garden.

Henry Sand scrambled to his feet again with a rapidity that seemed breathless for one of his bulk, and asked the man very angrily and abruptly what he was doing, at the same time telling him to clear out at once.

'Lord Stanes,' said the goblin of the garden, 'would be much obliged if Father Brown would come up to the house and speak to him.'

Henry Sand turned away furiously; but the priest put down his fury to the dislike that was known to exist between him and the nobleman in question. As they mounted the slope, Father Brown paused a moment as if tracing patterns on the smooth tree-trunk, glanced upwards once at the darker and more hidden hieroglyph said to be a record of romance; and then stared at the wider and more sprawling letters of the confession, or supposed confession of suicide.

'Do those letters remind you of anything?' he asked. And when his sulky companion shook his head, he added:

'They remind me of the writing on that placard that threatened him with the vengeance of the strikers.'

'This is the hardest riddle and the queerest tale I have ever tackled,' said Father Brown, a month later, as he sat opposite Lord Stanes in the recently furnished apartment of No. 188, the end flat which was the last to be finished before the interregnum of the industrial dispute and the transfer of work from the Trade Union. It was comfortably furnished; and Lord Stanes was presiding over grog and cigars, when the priest made his confession with a grimace. Lord Stanes had become rather surprisingly friendly, in a cool and casual way.

'I know that is saying a good deal, with your record,' said Stanes, 'but certainly the detectives, including our seductive friend with the glass eye, don't seem at all able to see the solution.'

Father Brown laid down his cigar and said carefully:

'It isn't that they can't see the solution. It is that they can't see the problem.'

'Indeed,' said the other, 'perhaps I can't see the problem either.'

'The problem is unlike all other problems, for this reason,' said Father Brown. 'It seems as if the criminal deliberately did two different things, either of which might have been successful; but which, when done together, could only defeat each other. I am assuming, what I firmly believe, that the same murderer pinned up the proclamation threatening a sort of Bolshevik murder, and also wrote on the tree confessing to an ordinary suicide. Now you may say it is after all possible that the proclamation was a proletarian proclamation; that some extremist workmen wanted to kill their employer, and killed him. Even if that were true, it would still stick at the mystery of why they left, or why anybody left, a contrary trail of private self-destruction. But it certainly isn't true. None of these workmen, however bitter, would have done a thing like that. I know them pretty well; I know their leaders quite well. To suppose that people like Tom Bruce or Hogan would assassinate somebody they could go for in the newspapers, and damage in all sorts of different ways, is the sort of psychology that sensible people call lunacy. No; there was somebody, who was not an indignant workman, who first played the part of an indignant workman, and then played the part of a suicidal employer. But, in the name of wonder, why? If he thought he could pass it off smoothly as a suicide, why did he first spoil it all by publishing a threat of murder? You might say it was an after-thought to fix up the suicide story, as less provocative than the murder story. But it wasn't less provocative *after* the murder story. He must have known he had already turned our thoughts towards murder, when it should have been his whole object to keep our thoughts away from it. If it was an after-thought, it was the after-thought of a very thoughtless person. And I have a notion that this assassin is a very thoughtful person. Can you make anything of it?'

'No; but I see what you mean,' said Stanes, 'by saying that I didn't even see the problem. It isn't merely who killed Sand;

it's why anybody should accuse somebody else of killing Sand and then accuse Sand of killing himself.'

Father Brown's face was knotted and the cigar was clenched in his teeth; the end of it glowed and darkened rhythmically like the signal of some burning pulse of the brain. Then he spoke as if to himself:

'We've got to follow very closely and very clearly. It's like separating threads of thought from each other; something like this. Because the murder charge really rather spoilt the suicide charge, he wouldn't normally have made the murder charge. But he did make it; so he had some other reason for making it. It was so strong a reason that perhaps it reconciled him even to weakening his other line of defence: that it was a suicide. In other words, the murder charge wasn't really a murder charge. I mean he wasn't using it as a murder charge, he wasn't doing it so as to shift to somebody else the guilt of murder; he was doing it for some other extraordinary reason of his own. His plan had to contain a proclamation that Sand would be murdered; whether it threw suspicion on other people or not. Somehow or other the mere proclamation itself was necessary. But why?'

He smoked and smouldered away with the same volcanic concentration for five minutes before he spoke again.

'What could a murderous proclamation do, besides suggesting that the strikers were the murderers? What *did* it do? One thing is obvious; it inevitably did the opposite of what it said. It told Sand not to lock out his men; and it was perhaps the only thing in the world that would really have made him do it. You've got to think of the sort of man and the sort of reputation. When a man has been called a Strong Man in our silly sensational newspapers, when he is fondly regarded as a Sportsman by all the most distinguished asses in England, he simply can't back down because he is threatened with a pistol. It would be like walking about at Ascot with a white feather stuck in his absurd white hat. It would break that inner idol or ideal of oneself, which every man not a downright dastard does really prefer to life. And Sand wasn't a dastard; he was courageous; he was also impulsive. It acted instantly like a charm; his nephew, who had been more or less mixed up with the workmen, cried out instantly that the threat must be absolutely and instantly defied.'

'Yes,' said Lord Stanes, 'I noticed that.' They looked at each other for an instant, and then Stanes added carelessly: 'So you think the thing the criminal really wanted was –'

'The Lock-out!' cried the priest energetically. 'The Strike or whatever you call it; the cessation of work, anyhow. He wanted the work to stop at once; perhaps the blacklegs to come in at once; certainly the Trade Unionists to go out at once. That is what he really wanted; God knows why. And he brought that off, I think, really without bothering much about its other implication of the existence of Bolshevist assassins. But then ... then I think something went wrong. I'm only guessing and groping very slowly here; but the only explanation I can think of is that something began to draw attention to the real seat of the trouble; to the reason, whatever it was, of his wanting to bring the building to a halt. And then belatedly, desperately, and rather inconsistently, he tried to lay the other trail that led to the river, simply and solely because it led away from the flats.'

He looked up through his moonlike spectacles, absorbing all the quality of the background and furniture; the restrained luxury of a quiet man of the world; and contrasting it with the two suitcases with which its occupant had arrived so recently in a newly-finished and quite unfurnished flat. Then he said rather abruptly:

'In short, the murderer was frightened of something or somebody in the flats. By the way, why did *you* come to live in the flats? ... Also by the way, young Henry told me you made an early appointment with him when you moved in. Is that true?'

'Not in the least,' said Stanes. 'I got the key from his uncle the night before. I've no notion why Henry came here that morning.'

'Ah,' said Father Brown, 'then I think I have some notion of why he came ... I *thought* you startled him by coming in just when he was coming out.'

'And yet,' said Stanes, looking across with a glitter in his grey-green eyes, 'you do rather think that I also am a mystery.'

'I think you are two mysteries,' said Father Brown. 'The first is why you originally retired from Sand's business. The second is why you have since come back to live in Sand's buildings.'

Stanes smoked reflectively, knocked out his ash, and rang a bell on the table before him. 'If you'll excuse me,' he said, 'I will summon two more to the council. Jackson, the little detective you know of, will answer the bell; and I've asked Henry Sand to come in a little later.'

Father Brown rose from his seat, walked across the room and looked down frowning into the fire-place.

'Meanwhile,' continued Stanes, 'I don't mind answering both your questions. I left the Sand business because I was sure there was some hanky-panky in it and somebody was pinching all the money. I came back to it, and took this flat, because I wanted to watch for the real truth about old Sand's death – on the spot.'

Father Brown faced round as the detective entered the room; he stood staring at the hearthrug and repeated: 'On the spot.'

'Mr Jackson will tell you,' said Stanes, 'that Sir Hubert commissioned him to find out who was the thief robbing the firm; and he brought a note of his discoveries the day before old Hubert disappeared.'

'Yes,' said Father Brown, 'and I know now where he disappeared to. I know where the body is.'

'Do you mean –?' began his host hastily.

'It is here,' said Father Brown, and stamped on the hearthrug. 'Here, under the elegant Persian rug in this cosy and comfortable room.'

'Where in the world did you find that?'

'I've just remembered,' said Father Brown, 'that I found it in my sleep.'

He closed his eyes as if trying to picture a dream, and went on dreamily:

'This is a murder story turning on the problem of How to Hide the Body; and I found it in my sleep. I was always woken up every morning by hammering from this building. On that morning I half-woke up, went to sleep again and woke once more, expecting to find it late; but it wasn't. Why? Because there *had*

137

been hammering that morning, though all the usual work had stopped; short, hurried hammering in the small hours before dawn. Automatically a man sleeping stirs at such a familiar sound. But he goes to sleep again, because the usual sound is not at the usual hour. Now why did a certain secret criminal want all the work to cease suddenly; and only new workers come in? Because, if the old workers had come in next day, they would have found a new piece of work done in the night. The old workers would have known where they left off; and they would have found the whole flooring of this room already nailed down. Nailed down by a man who knew how to do it; having mixed a good deal with the workmen and learned their ways.'

As he spoke, the door was pushed open and a head poked in with a thrusting motion; a small head at the end of a thick neck and a face that blinked at them through glasses.

'Henry Sand said,' observed Father Brown, staring at the ceiling, 'that he was no good at hiding things. But I think he did himself an injustice.'

Henry Sand turned and moved swiftly away down the corridor.

'He not only hid his thefts from the firm quite successfully for years,' went on the priest with an air of abstraction, 'but when his uncle discovered them, he hid his uncle's corpse in an entirely new and original manner.'

At the same instant Stanes again rang a bell, with a long strident steady ringing; and the little man with the glass eye was propelled or shot along the corridor after the fugitive, with something of the rotatory motion of a mechanical figure in a zoetrope. At the same moment, Father Brown looked out of the window, leaning over a small balcony, and saw five or six men start from behind bushes and railings in the street below and spread out equally mechanically like a fan or net; opening out after the fugitive who had shot like a bullet out of the front door. Father Brown saw only the pattern of the story; which had never strayed from that room; where Henry had strangled Hubert and hid his body under impenetrable flooring, stopping the whole work on the building to do it. A pin-prick had started his own suspicions; but only to tell him he had been led down the long loop of a lie. The point of the pin was that it was pointless.

He fancied he understood Stanes at last, and he liked to collect queer people who were difficult to understand. He realized that this tired gentleman, whom he had once accused of having green blood, had indeed a sort of cold green flame of conscientiousness or conventional honour, that had made him first shift out of a shady business, and then feel ashamed of having shifted it on to others; and come back as a bored laborious detective; pitching his camp on the very spot where the corpse had been buried; so that the murderer, finding him sniffing so near the corpse, had wildly staged the alternative drama of the dressing-gown and the drowned man. All that was plain enough, but, before he withdrew his head from the night air and the stars, Father Brown threw one glance upwards at the vast black bulk of the cyclopean building heaved far up into the night, and remembered Egypt and Babylon, and all that is at once eternal and ephemeral in the work of man.

'I was right in what I said first of all,' he said. 'It reminds one of Coppée's poem about the Pharaoh and the Pyramid. This house is supposed to be a hundred houses; and yet the whole mountain of building is only one man's tomb.'

EIGHT

The Insoluble Problem

THIS queer incident, in some ways perhaps the queerest of the many that came his way, happened to Father Brown at the time when his French friend Flambeau had retired from the profession of crime and had entered with great energy and success on the profession of crime investigator. It happened that both as a thief and a thief-taker, Flambeau had rather specialized in the matter of jewel thefts, on which he was admitted to be an expert, both in the matter of identifying jewels and the equally practical matter of identifying jewel-thieves. And it was in connection with his special knowledge of this subject, and a special commission which it had won for him, that he rang up his friend the priest on the particular morning on which this story begins.

Father Brown was delighted to hear the voice of his old friend, even on the telephone; but in a general way, and especially at that particular moment, Father Brown was not very fond of the telephone. He was one who preferred to watch people's faces and feel social atmospheres, and he knew well that without these things, verbal messages are apt to be very misleading, especially from total strangers. And it seemed as if, on that particular morning, a swarm of total strangers had been buzzing in his ear with more or less unenlightening verbal messages; the telephone seemed to be possessed of a demon of triviality. Perhaps the most distinctive voice was one which asked him whether he did not issue regular permits for murder and theft upon the payment of a regular tariff hung up in his church; and as the stranger, on being informed that this was not the case, concluded the colloquy with a hollow laugh, it may be presumed that he remained unconvinced. Then an agitated, rather inconsequent female voice rang up requesting him to come round at once to a certain hotel he had heard of some forty-five miles on the road to a neighbouring cathedral town; the request being immediately followed by a contradiction in the same voice, more agitated and yet more inconsequent, telling him that it did not matter and that he was not wanted after all. Then came an interlude of a Press agency asking him if he had anything to say on what a Film Actress had said about Moustaches for Men; and finally yet a third return of the agitated and inconsequent lady at the hotel, saying that he was wanted, after all. He vaguely supposed that this marked some of the hesitations and panics not unknown among those who are vaguely veering in the direction of Instruction, but he confessed to a considerable relief when the voice of Flambeau wound up the series with a hearty threat of immediately turning up to breakfast.

Father Brown very much preferred to talk to a friend sitting comfortably over a pipe, but it soon appeared that his visitor was on the warpath and full of energy, having every intention of carrying off the little priest captive on some important expedition of his own. It was true that there was a special circumstance involved which might be supposed to claim the priest's attention. Flambeau had figured several times of late as successfully thwarting a theft of famous precious stones; he had torn the tiara of the Duchess of Dulwich out of the very hand of the bandit as he bolted through the garden. He laid so ingenious a trap for the criminal who planned to carry off the celebrated Sapphire Necklace, that the artist in question actually carried off the copy which he had himself planned to leave as a substitute.

Such were doubtless the reasons that had led to his being specially summoned to guard the delivery of a rather different sort of treasure; perhaps even more valuable in its mere materials, but possessing also another sort of value. A world-famous reliquary, supposed to contain a relic of St. Dorothy the martyr, was to be delivered at the Catholic monastery in a cathedral town; and one of the most famous of international jewel-thieves was supposed to have an eye on it; or rather presumably on the gold and rubies of its setting, rather than its purely hagiological importance. Perhaps there was something in this association of ideas which made Flambeau feel that the priest would be a particularly appropriate companion in his adventure; but anyhow, he descended on him, breathing fire and ambition and very voluble about his plans for preventing the theft.

Flambeau indeed bestrode the priest's hearth gigantically and in the old swaggering musketeer attitude, twirling his great moustaches.

'You can't,' he cried, referring to the sixty-mile road to Casterbury. 'You can't allow a profane robbery like that to happen under your very nose.'

The relic was not to reach the monastery till the evening; and there was no need for its defenders to arrive earlier; for indeed a motor-journey would take them the greater part of the day. Moreover, Father Brown casually remarked that there was an inn on the road, at which he would prefer to lunch, as he had been already asked to look in there as soon as was convenient.

As they drove along through a densely wooded but sparsely inhabited landscape, in which inns and all other buildings seemed to grow rarer and rarer, the daylight began to take on the character of a stormy twilight even in the heat of noon; and dark purple clouds gathered over the dark grey forests. As is common under the lurid quietude of that kind of light, what colour there was in the landscape gained a sort of secretive glow which is not found in objects under the full sunlight; and ragged red leaves or golden or orange fungi seemed to burn with a dark fire of their own. Under such a half-light they came to a break in the woods like a great rent in a grey wall, and saw beyond, standing above the gap, the tall and rather outlandish-looking inn that bore the name of the Green Dragon.

The two old companions had often arrived together at inns and other human habitations, and found a somewhat singular state of things there; but the signs of singularity had seldom manifested themselves so early. For while their car was still some hundreds of yards from the dark green door, which matched the dark green shutters of the high and narrow building, the door was thrown open with violence and a woman with a wild mop of red hair rushed to meet them, as if she were ready to board the car in full career. Flambeau brought the car to a standstill, but almost before he had done so, she thrust her white and tragic face into the window, crying:

'Are you Father Brown?' and then almost in the same breath; 'who is this man?'

'This gentleman's name is Flambeau,' said Father Brown in a tranquil manner, 'and what can I do for you?'

'Come into the inn,' she said, with extraordinary abruptness even under the circumstances. 'There's been a murder done.'

They got out of the car in silence and followed her to the dark green door which opened inwards on a sort of dark green alley, formed of stakes and wooden pillars, wreathed with vine and ivy, showing square leaves of black and red and many sombre colours. This again led through an inner door into a sort of large parlour hung with rusty trophies of Cavalier arms, of which the furniture seemed to be antiquated and also in great confusion, like the inside of a lumber-room. They were quite startled for the moment; for it seemed as if one large piece of lumber rose and moved towards them; so dusty and shabby and ungainly was the man who thus abandoned what seemed like a state of permanent immobility.

Strangely enough, the man seemed to have a certain agility of politeness, when once he did move; even if it suggested the wooden joints of a courtly step-ladder or an obsequious towel-horse. Both Flambeau and Father Brown felt that they had hardly ever clapped eyes on a man who was so difficult to place. He was not what is called a gentleman; yet he had something of the dusty refinement of a scholar; there was something faintly disreputable or *déclassé* about him; and yet the smell of him was rather bookish than Bohemian. He was thin and pale, with a pointed nose and a dark pointed beard; his brow was bald, but his hair behind long and lank and stringy; and the expression of his eyes was almost entirely masked by a pair of blue spectacles. Father Brown felt that he had met something of the sort somewhere, and a long time ago; but he could no longer put a name to it. The lumber he sat among was largely literary lumber; especially bundles of seventeenth-century pamphlets.

'Do I understand the lady to say,' asked Flambeau gravely, 'that there is a murder here?'

The lady nodded her red ragged head rather impatiently; except for those flaming elf-locks she had lost some of her look of wildness; her dark dress was of a certain dignity and neatness; her features were strong and handsome; and there was something about her suggesting that double strength of body and mind which makes women powerful, particularly in contrast with men like the man in blue spectacles. Nevertheless, it was he who gave the only articulate answer, intervening with a certain antic gallantry.

'It is true that my unfortunate sister-in-law,' he explained, 'has almost this moment suffered a most appalling shock which we should all have desired to spare her. I only wish that I myself had made the discovery and suffered only the further distress of bringing the terrible news. Unfortunately it was Mrs Flood herself who found her aged grandfather, long sick and bedridden in this hotel, actually dead in the garden; in circumstances which point only too plainly to violence and assault. Curious circumstances, I may say, very curious circumstances indeed.' And he coughed slightly, as if apologizing for them.

Flambeau bowed to the lady and expressed his sincere sympathies; then he said to the man: 'I think you said, sir, that you are Mrs Flood's brother-in-law.'

'I am Dr Oscar Flood,' replied the other. 'My brother, this lady's husband, is at present away on the Continent on business, and she is running the hotel. Her grandfather was partially paralysed and very far advanced in years. He was never known to leave his bedroom; so that really these extraordinary circumstances...'

'Have you sent for a doctor or the police?' asked Flambeau.

'Yes,' replied Dr Flood, 'we rang up after making the dreadful discovery; but they can hardly be here for some hours. This roadhouse stands so very remote. It is only used by people going to Casterbury or even beyond. So we thought we might ask for your valuable assistance until –'

'If we are to be of any assistance,' said Father Brown, interrupting in too abstracted a manner to seem uncivil, 'I should say we had better go and look at the circumstances at once.'

He stepped almost mechanically towards the door; and almost

ran into a man who was shouldering his way in; a big, heavy young man with dark hair unbrushed and untidy, who would nevertheless have been rather handsome save for a slight disfigurement of one eye, which gave him rather a sinister appearance.

'What the devil are you doing?' he blurted out, 'telling every Tom, Dick and Harry – at least you ought to wait for the police.'

'I will be answerable to the police,' said Flambeau with a certain magnificence, and a sudden air of having taken command of everything. He advanced to the doorway, and as he was much bigger than the big young man, and his moustaches were as formidable as the horns of a Spanish bull, the big young man backed before him and had an inconsequent air of being thrown out and left behind, as the group swept out into the garden and up the flagged path towards the mulberry plantation. Only Flambeau heard the little priest say to the doctor: 'He doesn't seem to love us really, does he? By the way, who is he?'

'His name is Dunn,' said the doctor, with a certain restraint of manner. 'My sister-in-law gave him the job of managing the garden, because he lost an eye in the War.'

As they went through the mulberry bushes, the landscape of the garden presented that rich yet ominous effect which is found when the land is actually brighter than the sky. In the broken sunlight from behind, the tree-tops in front of them stood up like pale green flames against a sky steadily blackening with storm, through every shade of purple and violet. The same light struck strips of the lawn and garden beds; and whatever it illuminated seemed more mysteriously sombre and secret for the light. The garden bed was dotted with tulips that looked like drops of dark blood, and some of which one might have sworn were truly black; and the line ended appropriately with a tulip tree; which Father Brown was disposed, if partly by some confused memory, to identify with what is commonly called the Judas tree. What assisted the association was the fact that there was hanging from one of the branches, like a dried fruit, the dry, thin body of an old man, with a long beard that wagged grotesquely in the wind.

There lay on it something more than the horror of darkness,

the horror of sunlight; for the fitful sun painted tree and man in gay colours like a stage property; the tree was in flower and the corpse was hung with a faded peacock-green dressing-gown, and wore on its wagging head a scarlet smoking-cap. Also it had red bedroom-slippers, one of which had fallen off and lay on the grass like a blot of blood.

But neither Flambeau or Father Brown was looking at these things as yet. They were both staring at a strange object that seemed to stick out of the middle of the dead man's shrunken figure; and which they gradually perceived to be the black but rather rusty iron hilt of a seventeenth-century sword, which had completely transfixed the body. They both remained almost motionless as they gazed at it; until the restless Dr Flood seemed to grow quite impatient with their stolidity.

'What puzzles *me* most,' he said, nervously snapping his fingers, 'is the actual state of the body. And yet it has given me an idea already.'

Flambeau had stepped up to the tree and was studying the sword-hilt through an eye-glass. But for some odd reason, it was at that very instant that the priest in sheer perversity spun round like a teetotum, turned his back on the corpse, and looked peeringly in the very opposite direction. He was just in time to see the red head of Mrs Flood at the remote end of the garden, turned towards a dark young man, too dim with distance to be identified, who was at that moment mounting a motor-bicycle; who vanished, leaving behind him only the dying din of that vehicle. Then the woman turned and began to walk towards them across the garden, just as Father Brown turned also and began a careful inspection of the sword-hilt and the hanging corpse.

'I understand you only found him about half an hour ago,' said Flambeau. 'Was there anybody about here just before that? I mean anybody in his bedroom, or that part of the house, or this part of the garden – say for an hour beforehand?'

'No,' said the doctor with precision. 'That is the very tragic accident. My sister-in-law was in the pantry, which is a sort of out-house on the other side; this man Dunn was in the kitchen-garden, which is also in that direction; and I myself was poking about among the books, in a room just behind the one you found me in. There are two female servants, but one had gone to the post and the other was in the attic.'

'And were any of these people,' asked Flambeau, very quietly, 'I say *any* of these people, at all on bad terms with the poor old gentleman?'

'He was the object of almost universal affection,' replied the doctor solemnly. 'If there were any misunderstandings, they were mild and of a sort common in modern times. The old man was attached to the old religious habits; and perhaps his daughter and son-in-law had rather wider views. All that can have had nothing to do with a ghastly and fantastic assassination like this.'

'It depends on how wide the modern views were,' said Father Brown, 'or how narrow.'

At this moment they heard Mrs Flood hallooing across the garden as she came, and calling her brother-in-law to her with a certain impatience. He hurried towards her and was soon out of earshot; but as he went he waved his hand apologetically and then pointed with a long finger to the ground.

'You will find the footprints very intriguing,' he said; with the same strange air, as of a funereal showman.

The two amateur detectives looked across at each other. 'I find several other things intriguing,' said Flambeau.

'Oh, yes,' said the priest, staring rather foolishly at the grass.

'I was wondering,' said Flambeau, 'why they should hang a man by the neck till he was dead, and then take the trouble to stick him with a sword.'

'And I was wondering,' said Father Brown, 'why they should kill a man with a sword thrust through his heart, and then take the trouble to hang him by the neck.'

'Oh, you are simply being contrary,' protested his friend. 'I can see at a glance that they didn't stab him alive. The body would have bled more and the wound wouldn't have closed like that.'

'And I could see at a glance,' said Father Brown, peering up very awkwardly, with his short stature and short sight, 'that they didn't hang him alive. If you'll look at the knot in the noose, you will see it's tied so clumsily that a twist of rope holds it away from the neck, so that it couldn't throttle a man at all. He was dead before they put the rope on him; and he was dead before they put the sword in him. And how was he really killed?'

'I think,' remarked the other, 'that we'd better go back to the house and have a look at his bedroom – and other things.'

'So we will,' said Father Brown. 'But among other things perhaps we had better have a look at these footprints. Better begin at the other end, I think, by his window. Well, there are no footprints on the paved path, as there might be; but then again there mightn't be. Well, here is the lawn just under his bedroom window. And here are his footprints plain enough.'

He blinked ominously at the footprints; and then began carefully retracing his path towards the tree, every now and then ducking in an undignified manner to look at something on the ground. Eventually he returned to Flambeau and said in a chatty manner:

'Well, do you know the story that is written there very plainly? Though it's not exactly a plain story.'

'I wouldn't be content to call it plain,' said Flambeau. 'I should call it quite ugly.'

'Well,' said Father Brown, 'the story that is stamped quite plainly on the earth, with exact moulds of the old man's slippers, is this. The aged paralytic leapt from the window and ran down the beds parallel to the path, quite eager for all the fun of being strangled and stabbed; so eager that he hopped on one leg out of sheer lightheartedness; and even occasionally turned cart-wheels –'

'Stop!' cried Flambeau, angrily. 'What the hell is all this hellish pantomime?'

Father Brown merely raised his eyebrows and gestured mildly towards the hieroglyphs in the dust. 'About half the way there's only the mark of one slipper; and in some places the mark of a hand planted all by itself.'

'Couldn't he have limped and then fallen?' asked Flambeau.

Father Brown shook his head. 'At least he'd have tried to use his hands and feet, or knees and elbows, in getting up. There are no other marks there of any kind. Of course the flagged path is quite near, and there are no marks on that; though there might be on the soil between the cracks: it's a crazy pavement.'

'By God, it's a crazy pavement; and a crazy garden; and a crazy story!' And Flambeau looked gloomily across the gloomy and storm-stricken garden, across which the crooked patchwork paths did indeed give a queer aptness to the quaint old English adjective.

'And now,' said Father Brown, 'let us go up and look at his room.' They went in by a door not far from the bedroom window; and the priest paused a moment to look at an ordinary garden broomstick, for sweeping up leaves, that was leaning against the wall. 'Do you see that?'

'It's a broomstick,' said Flambeau, with solid irony.

'It's a blunder,' said Father Brown; 'the first blunder that I've seen in this curious plot.'

They mounted the stairs and entered the old man's bedroom; and a glance at it made fairly clear the main facts, both about the foundation and disunion of the family. Father Brown had felt from the first that he was in what was, or had been, a Catholic household; but was, at least partly, inhabited by lapsed or very loose Catholics. The pictures and images in the grandfather's room made it clear that what positive piety remained had been practically confined to him; and that his kindred had, for some reason or other, gone Pagan. But he agreed that this was a hopelessly inadequate explanation even of an ordinary murder; let alone such a very extraordinary murder as this. 'Hang it all,' he muttered, 'the murder is really the least extra-ordinary part of it.' And even as he used the chance phrase, a slow light began to dawn upon his face.

Flambeau had seated himself on a chair by the little table which stood beside the dead man's bed. He was frowning thoughtfully at three or four white pills or pellets that lay in a small tray beside a bottle of water.

'The murderer or murderess,' said Flambeau, 'had some incomprehensible reason or other for wanting us to think the dead man was strangled or stabbed or both. He was not strangled or stabbed or anything of the kind. Why did they want to suggest it? The most logical explanation is that he died in some particular way which would, in itself, suggest a connection with some particular person. Suppose, for instance, he was poisoned. And suppose somebody is involved who would naturally look more like a poisoner than anybody else.'

'After all,' said Father Brown softly, 'our friend in the blue spectacles is a doctor.'

'I'm going to examine these pills pretty carefully,' went on Flambeau. 'I don't want to lose them, though. They look as if they were soluble in water.'

'It may take you some time to do anything scientific with them,' said the priest, 'and the police doctor may be here before that. So I should certainly advise you not to lose them. That is, if you are going to wait for the police doctor.'

'I am going to stay here till I have solved this problem,' said Flambeau.

'Then you will stay here for ever,' said Father Brown, looking calmly out of the window. 'I don't think I shall stay in this room, anyhow.'

'Do you mean that I shan't solve the problem?' asked his friend. 'Why shouldn't I solve the problem?'

'Because it isn't soluble in water. No, nor in blood,' said the priest; and he went down the dark stairs into the darkening garden. There he saw again what he had already seen from the window.

The heat and weight and obscurity of the thunderous sky seemed to be pressing yet more closely on the landscape; the clouds had conquered the sun which, above, in a narrowing clearance, stood up paler than the moon. There was a thrill of thunder in the air, but now no more stirring of wind or breeze; and even the colours of the garden seemed only like richer shades of darkness. But one colour still glowed with a certain dusky vividness; and that was the red hair of the woman of that house, who was standing with a sort of rigidity, staring, with her hands thrust up into her hair. That scene of eclipse, with something deeper in his own doubts about its significance, brought to the surface the memory of haunting and mystical lines; and he found himself murmuring: 'A secret spot, as savage and enchanted as e'er beneath a waning moon was haunted by woman wailing for her demon lover.' His muttering became more agitated. 'Holy Mary, Mother of God, pray for us sinners ... that's what it is; that's terribly like what it is; *woman wailing for her demon lover.*'

He was hesitant and almost shaky as he approached the woman; but he spoke with his common composure. He was gazing at her very steadily, as he told her earnestly that she must not be morbid because of the mere accidental accessories of the tragedy, with all their mad ugliness. 'The pictures in your grandfather's room were truer to him than that ugly picture that we saw,' he said gravely. 'Something tells me he was a good man; and it does not matter what his murderers did with his body.'

'Oh, I am sick of his holy pictures and statues!' she said, turning her head away. 'Why don't they defend themselves, if they are what you say they are? But rioters can knock off the Blessed Virgin's head and nothing happens to them. Oh, what's the good? You can't blame us, you daren't blame us, if we've found out that Man is stronger than God.'

'Surely,' said Father Brown very gently, 'it is not generous to make even God's patience with us a point against Him.'

'God may be patient and Man impatient,' she answered, 'and suppose we like the impatience better. You call it sacrilege; but you can't stop it.'

Father Brown gave a curious little jump. 'Sacrilege!' he said; and suddenly turned back to the doorway with a new brisk air of decision. At the same moment Flambeau appeared in the doorway, pale with excitement, with a screw of paper in his hands. Father Brown had already opened his mouth to speak, but his impetuous friend spoke before him.

'I'm on the track at last!' cried Flambeau. 'These pills look the same, but they're really different. And do you know that, at the very moment I spotted them, that one-eyed brute of a gardener thrust his white face into the room; and he was carrying a horse-pistol. I knocked it out of his hand and threw him down the stairs, but I begin to understand everything. If I stay here another hour or two, I shall finish my job.'

'Then you will not finish it,' said the priest, with a ring in his voice very rare in him indeed. 'We shall not stay here another hour. We shall not stay here another minute. We must leave this place at once!'

'What!' cried the astounded Flambeau. 'Just when we are getting near the truth! Why, you can tell that we're getting near the truth because they are afraid of us.'

Father Brown looked at him with a stony and inscrutable face, and said:

They are not afraid of us when we are here. They will only be afraid of us when we are not here.'

'They had both become conscious that the rather fidgety figure of Dr Flood was hovering in the lurid haze; now it precipitated itself forward with the wildest gestures.

'Stop! Listen!' cried the agitated doctor. 'I have discovered the truth!'

'Then you can explain it to your own police,' said Father Brown, briefly. 'They ought to be coming soon. But we must be going.'

The doctor seemed thrown into a whirlpool of emotions, eventually rising to the surface again with a despairing cry. He spread out his arms like a cross, barring their way.

'Be it so!' he cried. 'I will not deceive you now, by saying I have discovered the truth. I will only confess the truth.'

'Then you can confess it to your own priest,' said Father Brown, and strode towards the garden gate, followed by his staring friend. Before he reached the gate, another figure had rushed athwart him like the wind; and Dunn the gardener was shouting at him some unintelligible derision at detectives who were running away from their job. Then the priest ducked just in time to dodge a blow from the horse-pistol, wielded like a club. But Dunn was just not in time to dodge a blow from the fist of Flambeau, which was like the club of Hercules. The two left Mr Dunn spread flat behind them on the path, and, passing out of the gate, went out and got into their car in silence. Flambeau only asked one brief question and Father Brown only answered: 'Casterbury.'

At last, after a long silence, the priest observed: 'I could almost believe the storm belonged only to that garden, and came out of a storm in the soul.'

'My friend,' said Flambeau, 'I have known you a long time, and when you show certain signs of certainty, I follow your lead. But I hope you are not going to tell me that you took me away from that fascinating job, because you did not like the atmosphere.'

'Well, it was certainly a terrible atmosphere,' replied Father Brown, calmly. 'Dreadful and passionate and oppressive. And the most dreadful thing about it was this – that there was no hate in it at all.'

'Somebody,' suggested Flambeau, 'seems to have had a slight dislike of grandpapa.'

'Nobody had any dislike of anybody,' said Father Brown with a groan. 'That was the dreadful thing in that darkness. It was love.'

'Curious way of expressing love – to strangle somebody and stick him with a sword,' observed the other.

'It was love,' repeated the priest, 'and it filled the house with terror.'

'Don't tell me,' protested Flambeau, 'that that beautiful woman is in love with that spider in spectacles.'

'No,' said Father Brown and groaned again. 'She is in love with her husband. It is ghastly.'

'It is a state of things that I have often heard you recommend,' replied Flambeau. 'You cannot call that lawless love.'

'Not lawless in that sense,' answered Father Brown; then he turned sharply on his elbow and spoke with a new warmth: 'Do you think I don't know that the love of a man and a woman was the first command of God and is glorious for ever? Are you one of those idiots who think we don't admire love and marriage? Do I need to be told of the Garden of Eden or the wine of Cana? It is just because the strength in the thing was the strength of God, that it rages with that awful energy even when it breaks loose from God. When the Garden becomes a jungle, but still a glorious jungle; when the second fermentation turns the wine of Cana into the vinegar of Calvary. Do you think I don't know all that?'

'I'm sure you do,' said Flambeau, 'but I don't yet know much about my problem of the murder.'

'The murder cannot be solved,' said Father Brown.

'And why not?' demanded his friend.

'Because there is no murder to solve,' said Father Brown.

Flambeau was silent with sheer surprise; and it was his friend who resumed in a quiet tone:

'I'll tell you a curious thing. I talked with that woman when she was wild with grief; but she never said anything about the murder. She never mentioned murder, or even alluded to murder. What she did mention repeatedly was sacrilege.'

Then, with another jerk of verbal disconnection, he added: 'Have you ever heard of Tiger Tyrone?'

'Haven't I!' cried Flambeau. 'Why, that's the very man who's supposed to be after the reliquary, and whom I've been commissioned specially to circumvent. He's the most violent and daring gangster who ever visited this country; Irish, of course, but the sort that goes quite crazily anti-clerical. Perhaps he's dabbled in a little diabolism in these secret societies; anyhow, he has a macabre taste for playing all sorts of wild tricks that look wickeder than they are. Otherwise he's not the wickedest; he seldom kills, and never for cruelty; but he loves doing anything to shock people, especially his own people; robbing churches or digging up skeletons or what not.'

'Yes,' said Father Brown, 'it all fits in. I ought to have seen it all long before.'

'I don't see how we could have seen anything, after only an hour's investigation,' said the detective defensively.

'I ought to have seen it before there was anything to investigate,' said the priest. 'I ought to have known it before you arrived this morning.'

'What on earth do you mean?'

'It only shows how wrong voices sound on the telephone,' said Father Brown reflectively. 'I heard all three stages of the thing this morning; and I thought they were trifles. First, a woman rang me up and asked me to go to that inn as soon as possible. What did that mean? Of course it meant that the old grandfather was dying. Then she rang up to say that I needn't go, after all. What did that mean? Of course it meant that the old grandfather was dead. He had died quite peaceably in his bed; probably heart failure from sheer old age. And then she rang up a third time and said I was to go, after all. What did that mean? Ah, that is rather more interesting!'

He went on after a moment's pause: 'Tiger Tyrone, whose wife worships him, took hold of one of his mad ideas, and yet it was a crafty idea, too. He had just heard that you were tracking him down, that you knew him and his methods and were coming to save the reliquary; he may have heard that I have sometimes been of some assistance. He wanted to stop us on the road; and his trick for doing it was to stage a murder. It was a pretty horrible thing to do; but it wasn't a murder. Probably he bullied his wife with an air of brutal common sense, saying he could only escape penal servitude by using a dead body that couldn't suffer anything from such use. Anyhow, his wife would do anything for him; but she felt all the unnatural hideousness of that hanging masquerade; and that's why she talked about sacrilege. She was thinking of the desecration of the relic; but also of the desecration of the death-bed. The brother's one of those shoddy "scientific" rebels who tinker with dud bombs; an idealist run to seed. But he's devoted to Tiger; and so is the gardener. Perhaps it's a point in his favour that so many people seem devoted to him.

'There was one little point that set me guessing very early. Among the old books the doctor was turning over, was a bundle of seventeenth-century pamphlets; and I caught one title: *True Declaration of the Trial and Execution of My Lord Stafford.* Now Stafford was executed in the Popish Plot business, which began with one of history's detective stories; the death of Sir Edmund Berry Godfrey. Godfrey was found dead in a ditch, and part of the mystery was that he had marks of strangulation, but was also transfixed with his own sword. I thought at once that somebody in the house might have got the idea from here. But he couldn't have wanted it as a way of committing a murder. He can only have wanted it as a way of creating a mystery. Then I saw that this applied to all the other outrageous details. They were devilish enough; but it wasn't mere devilry; there was a rag of excuse; because they had to make the mystery as contradictory and complicated as possible, to make sure that we should be a long time solving it – or rather seeing through it. So they dragged the poor old man off his deathbed and made the corpse hop and turn cartwheels and do everything that it *couldn't* have done. They had to give us an Insoluble Problem. They swept their own tracks off the path, leaving the broom. Fortunately we did see through it in time.'

'You saw through it in time,' said Flambeau. 'I might have lingered a little longer over the second trail they left, sprinkled with assorted pills.'

'Well, anyhow, we got away,' said Father Brown, comfortably.

'And that, I presume,' said Flambeau, 'is the reason I am driving at this rate along the road to Casterbury.'

That night in the monastery and church at Casterbury there were events calculated to stagger monastic seclusion. The reliquary of St Dorothy, in a casket gorgeous with gold and rubies, was temporarily placed in a side room near the chapel of the monastery, to be brought in with a procession for a special service at the end of Benediction. It was guarded for the moment by one monk, who watched it in a tense and vigilant manner; for he and his brethren knew all about the shadow of peril from the prowling of Tiger Tyrone. Thus it was that the monk was on his feet in a flash, when he saw one of the low-latticed windows beginning to open and a dark object crawling like a black serpent through the crack. Rushing across, he gripped it and found it was the arm and sleeve of a man, terminating with a handsome cuff and a smart dark-grey glove. Laying hold of it, he shouted for help, and even as he did so, a man darted into the room through the door behind his back and snatched the casket he had left behind him on the table. Almost at the same instant, the arm wedged in the window came away in his hand, and he stood holding the stuffed limb of a dummy.

Tiger Tyrone had played that trick before, but to the monk it was a novelty. Fortunately, there was at least one person to whom the Tiger's tricks were not a novelty; and that person appeared with militant moustaches, gigantically framed in the doorway, at the very moment when the Tiger turned to escape by it. Flambeau and Tiger Tyrone looked at each other with steady eyes and exchanged something that was almost like a military salute.

Meanwhile Father Brown had slipped into the chapel, to say a prayer for several persons involved in these unseemly events. But he was rather smiling than otherwise, and, to tell the truth, he was not by any means hopeless about Mr Tyrone and his deplorable family; but rather more hopeful than he was for many more respectable people. Then his thoughts widened with the grander perspectives of the place and the occasion. Against black and green marbles at the end of the rather rococo chapel, the dark-red vestments of the festival of a martyr were in their turn a background for a fierier red; a red like red-hot coals: the rubies of the reliquary; the roses of St Dorothy. And he had again a thought to throw back to the strange events of that day, and the woman who had shuddered at the sacrilege she had helped. After all, he thought, St Dorothy also had a Pagan lover; but he had not dominated her or destroyed her faith. She had died free and for the truth; and then had sent him roses from Paradise...

He raised his eyes and saw through the veil of incense smoke and of twinkling lights that Benediction was drawing to its end while the procession waited. The sense of accumulated riches of time and tradition pressed past him like a crowd moving in rank after rank, through unending centuries; and high above them all, like a garland of unfading flames, like the sun of our mortal midnight, the great monstrance blazed against the darkness of the vaulted shadows, as it blazed against the black enigma of the universe. For some are convinced that this enigma also is an Insoluble Problem. And others have equal certitude that it has but one solution.

NINE

The Vampire of the Village

AT the twist of a path in the hills, where two poplars stood up like pyramids dwarfing the tiny village of Potter's Pond, a mere huddle of houses, there once walked a man in a costume of a very conspicuous cut and colour, wearing a vivid magenta coat and a white hat tilted upon black ambrosial curls, which ended with a sort of Byronic flourish of whisker.

The riddle of why he was wearing clothes of such fantastic antiquity, yet wearing them with an air of fashion and even swagger, was but one of the many riddles that were eventually solved in solving the mystery of his fate. The point here is that when he had passed the poplars he seemed to have vanished; as if he had faded into the wan and widening dawn or been blown away upon the wind of morning.

It was only about a week afterwards that his body was found a quarter of a mile away, broken upon the steep rockeries of a terraced garden leading up to a gaunt and shuttered house called The Grange. Just before he had vanished, he had been accidentally overheard apparently quarrelling with some by-standers, and especially abusing their village as 'a wretched little hamlet'; and it was supposed that he had aroused some extreme passions of local patriotism and eventually been their victim. At least the local doctor testified that the skull had suffered a crushing blow that might have caused death, though probably only inflicted with some sort of club or cudgel. This fitted in well enough with the notion of an attack by rather savage yokels. But nobody ever found any means of tracing any particular yokel; and the inquest returned a verdict of murder by some persons unknown.

A year or two afterwards the question was re-opened in a curious way; a series of events which led a certain Dr Mulborough, called by his intimates Mulberry in apt allusion to something rich and fruity about his dark rotundity and rather empurpled visage, travelling by train down to Potter's Pond, with a friend whom he had often consulted upon problems of the kind. In spite of the somewhat port-winy and ponderous exterior of the doctor, he had a shrewd eye and was really a man of very remarkable sense; which he considered that he showed in consulting a little priest named Brown, whose acquaintance he had made over a poisoning case long ago. The little priest was sitting opposite to him, with the air of a patient baby absorbing instruction; and the doctor was explaining at length the real reasons for the journey.

'I cannot agree with the gentleman in the magenta coat that Potter's Pond is only a wretched little hamlet. But it is certainly a very remote and secluded village; so that it seems quite outlandish, like a village of a hundred years ago. The spinsters are really spinsters – damn it, you could almost imagine you saw them spin. The ladies are not just ladies. They are gentlewomen; and their chemist is not a chemist, but an apothecary; pronounced potecary. They do just admit the existence of an ordinary doctor like myself to assist the apothecary. But I am considered rather a juvenile innovation, because I am only fifty-seven years old and have only been in the county for twenty-eight years. The solicitor looks as if he had known it for twenty-eight thousand years. Then there is the old Admiral, who is just like a Dickens illustration; with a house full of cutlasses and cuttle-fish and equipped with a telescope.'

'I suppose,' said Father Brown, 'there are always a certain number of Admirals washed up on the shore. But I never understood why they get stranded so far inland.'

'Certainly no dead-alive place in the depths of the country is complete without one of these little creatures,' said the doctor. 'And then, of course, there is the proper sort of clergyman; Tory and High Church in a dusty fashion dating from Archbishop Laud; more of an old woman than any of the old women. He's a white-haired studious old bird, more easily shocked than the spinsters. Indeed, the gentlewomen, though Puritan in their principles, are sometimes pretty plain in their speech; as the real Puritans were. Once or twice I have known old Miss Carstairs-Carew use expressions as lively as anything in the Bible. The dear old clergyman is assiduous in reading the Bible; but I almost fancy he shuts his eyes when he comes to those words. Well, you know I'm not particularly modern. I don't enjoy this jazzing and joy-riding of the Bright Young Things –'

'The Bright Young Things don't enjoy it,' said Father Brown. 'That is the real tragedy.'

'But I am naturally rather more in touch with the world than the people in this prehistoric village,' pursued the doctor. 'And I had reached a point when I almost welcomed the Great Scandal.'

'Don't say the Bright Young Things have found Potter's Pond after all,' observed the priest, smiling.

'Oh, even our scandal is on old-established melodramatic lines. Need I say that the clergyman's son promises to be our problem? It would be almost irregular, if the clergyman's son were quite regular. So far as I can see, he is very mildly and almost feebly irregular. He was first seen drinking ale outside the Blue Lion. Only it seems he is a poet, which in those parts is next door to being a poacher.'

'Surely,' said Father Brown, 'even in Potter's Pond that cannot be the Great Scandal.'

'No,' replied the doctor gravely. 'The Great Scandal began thus. In the house called The Grange, situated at the extreme end of The Grove, there lives a lady. A Lonely Lady. She calls herself Mrs Maltravers (that is how we put it); but she only came a year or two ago and nobody knows anything about her. "I can't think why she wants to live here," said Miss Carstairs-Carew; "we do not visit her."'

'Perhaps that's why she wants to live there,' said Father Brown.

'Well, her seclusion is considered suspicious. She annoys them by being good-looking and even what is called good style. And all the young men are warned against her as a vamp.'

'People who lose all their charity generally lose all their logic,' remarked Father Brown. 'It's rather ridiculous to complain that

160

she keeps herself to herself; and then accuse her of vamping the whole male population.'

'That is true,' said the doctor. 'And yet she is really rather a puzzling person. I saw her and found her intriguing; one of those brown women, long and elegant and beautifully ugly, if you know what I mean. She is rather witty, and though young enough certainly gives me an impression of what they call – well, experience. What the old ladies call a Past.'

'All the old ladies having been born this very minute,' observed Father Brown. 'I think I can assume she is supposed to have vamped the parson's son.'

'Yes, and it seems to be a very awful problem to the poor old parson. She is supposed to be a widow.'

Father Brown's face had a flash and spasm of his rare irritation. 'She is supposed to be a widow, as the parson's son is supposed to be the parson's son, and the solicitor is supposed to be a solicitor and you are supposed to be a doctor. Why in thunder shouldn't she be a widow? Have they one speck of *prima facie* evidence for doubting that she is what she says she is?'

Dr Mulborough abruptly squared his broad shoulders and sat up.

'Of course you're right again,' he said. 'But we haven't come to the scandal yet. Well, the scandal is that she is a widow.'

'Oh,' said Father Brown; and his face altered and he said something soft and faint, that might almost have been 'My God!'

'First of all,' said the doctor, 'they have made one discovery about Mrs Maltravers. She is an actress.'

'I fancied so,' said Father Brown. 'Never mind why. I had another fancy about her, that would seem even more irrelevant.'

'Well, at that instant it was scandal enough that she was an actress. The dear old clergyman of course is heartbroken, to think that his white hairs should be brought in sorrow to the grave by an actress and adventuress. The spinsters shriek in chorus. The Admiral admits he has sometimes been to a theatre in town; but objects to such things in what he calls "our midst". Well, of course I've no particular objections of that kind. This actress is certainly a lady, if a bit of a Dark Lady, in the manner of the

161

Sonnets; the young man is very much in love with her; and I am
no doubt a sentimental old fool in having a sneaking sympathy
with the misguided youth who is sneaking round the Moated
Grange; and I was getting into quite a pastoral frame of mind
about this idyll, when suddenly the thunderbolt fell. And I,
who am the only person who ever had any sympathy with these
people, am sent down to be the messenger of doom.'

'Yes,' said Father Brown, 'and why *were* you sent down?'

The doctor answered with a sort of groan:

'Mrs Maltravers is not only a widow, but she is the widow of
Mr Maltravers.'

'It sounds a shocking revelation, as you state it,' acknowledged
the priest seriously.

'And Mr Maltravers,' continued his medical friend, 'was the
man who was apparently murdered in this very village a year
or two ago; supposed to have been bashed on the head by one
of the simple villagers.'

'I remember you told me,' said Father Brown. 'The doctor,
or some doctor, said he had probably died of being clubbed on
the head with a cudgel.'

Dr Mulborough was silent for a moment in frowning embarrassment, and then said curtly:

'Dog doesn't eat dog, and doctors don't bite doctors, not even
when they are mad doctors. I shouldn't care to cast any reflection
on my eminent predecessor in Potter's Pond, if I could avoid it;
but I know you are really safe for secrets. And, speaking in
confidence, my eminent predecessor at Potter's Pond was a
blasted fool; a drunken old humbug and absolutely incompetent.
I was asked, originally by the Chief Constable of the County
(for I've lived a long time in the county, though only recently in
the village), to look into the whole business; the depositions
and reports of the inquest and so on. And there simply isn't
any question about it. Maltravers may have been hit on the head;
he was a strolling actor passing through the place; and Potter's
Pond probably thinks it is all in the natural order that such people
should be hit on the head. But whoever hit him on the head did
not kill him; it is simply impossible for the injury, as described,
to do more than knock him out for a few hours. But lately I have

managed to turn up some other facts bearing on the matter; and the result of it is pretty grim.'

He sat louring at the landscape as it slid past the window, and then said more curtly:

'I am coming down here, and asking your help, because there's going to be an exhumation. There is very strong suspicion of poison.'

'And here we are at the station,' said Father Brown cheerfully. 'I suppose your idea is that poisoning the poor man would naturally fall among the household duties of his wife.'

'Well, there never seems to have been anyone else here who had any particular connection with him,' replied Mulborough, as they alighted from the train. 'At least there is one queer old crony of his, a broken-down actor, hanging around; but the police and the local solicitor seem convinced he is an unbalanced busybody; with some *idée fixe* about a quarrel with an actor who was his enemy; but who certainly wasn't Maltravers. A wandering accident, I should say, and certainly nothing to do with the problem of the poison.'

Father Brown had heard the story. But he knew that he never knew a story until he knew the characters in the story. He spent the next two or three days in going the rounds, on one polite excuse or another, to visit the chief actors of the drama. His first interview with the mysterious widow was brief but bright. He brought away from it at least two facts; one that Mrs Maltravers sometimes talked in a way which the Victorian village would call cynical; and, second, that like not a few actresses, she happened to belong to his own religious communion.

He was not so illogical (nor so unorthodox) as to infer from this alone that she was innocent of the alleged crime. He was well aware that his old religious communion could boast of several distinguished poisoners. But he had no difficulty in understanding its connection, in this sort of case, with a certain intellectual liberty which these Puritans would call laxity; and which would certainly seem to this parochial patch of an older England to be almost cosmopolitan. Anyhow, he was sure she could count for a great deal, whether for good or evil. Her brown eyes were brave to the point of battle, and her enigmatic mouth, humorous and rather large, suggested that her purposes touching the parson's poetical son, whatever they might be, were planted pretty deep.

The parson's poetical son himself, interviewed amid vast village scandal on a bench outside the Blue Lion, gave an impression of pure sulks. Hurrel Horner, a son of the Rev. Samuel Horner, was a square-built young man in a pale grey suit with a touch of something arty in a pale green tie, otherwise mainly notable for a mane of auburn hair and a permanent scowl. But Father Brown had a way with him in getting people to explain at considerable length why they refused to say a single word. About the general scandalmongering in the village, the young man began to curse freely. He even added a little scandalmongering of his own. He referred bitterly to alleged past flirtations between the Puritan Miss Carstairs-Carew and Mr Carver the solicitor. He even accused that legal character of having attempted to force himself upon the acquaintance of Mrs Maltravers. But when he came to speak of his own father, whether out of an acid decency or piety, or because his anger was too deep for speech, he snapped out only a few words.

'Well, there it is. He denounces her day and night as a painted adventuress; a sort of barmaid with gilt hair. I tell him she's not; you've met her yourself, and you know she's not. But he won't even meet her. He won't even see her in the street or look at her out of a window. An actress would pollute his house and even his holy presence. If he is called a Puritan he says he's proud to be a Puritan.'

'Your father,' said Father Brown, 'is entitled to have his views respected, whatever they are; they are not views I understand very well myself. But I agree he is not entitled to lay down the law about a lady he has never seen and then refuse even to look at her, to see if he is right. That is illogical.'

'That's his very stiffest point,' replied the youth. 'Not even one momentary meeting. Of course, he thunders against my other theatrical tastes as well.'

Father Brown swiftly followed up the new opening, and learnt much that he wanted to know. The alleged poetry, which was such a blot on the young man's character, was almost entirely dramatic poetry. He had written tragedies in verse which had been admired by good judges. He was no mere stage-struck fool; indeed he was no fool of any kind. He had some really original ideas about acting Shakespeare; it was easy to understand his having been dazzled and delighted by finding the brilliant lady at the Grange. And even the priest's intellectual sympathy so far mellowed the rebel of Potter's Pond that at their parting he actually smiled.

It was that smile which suddenly revealed to Father Brown that the young man was really miserable. So long as he frowned, it might well have been only sulks; but when he smiled it was somehow a more real revelation of sorrow.

Something continued to haunt the priest about that interview with the poet. An inner instinct certified that the sturdy young man was eaten from within, by some grief greater even than the conventional story of conventional parents being obstacles to the course of true love. It was all the more so, because there were not any obvious alternative causes. The boy was already rather a literary and dramatic success; his books might be said to be booming. Nor did he drink or dissipate his well-earned wealth. His notorious revels at the Blue Lion reduced themselves to one glass of light ale; and he seemed to be rather careful with his money. Father Brown thought of another possible complication in connection with Hurrel's large resources and small expenditure; and his brow darkened.

The conversation of Miss Carstairs-Carew, on whom he called next, was certainly calculated to paint the parson's son in the darkest colours. But as it was devoted to blasting him with all the special vices which Father Brown was quite certain the young man did not exhibit, he put it down to a common combination of Puritanism and gossip. The lady, though lofty, was quite gracious, however, and offered the visitor a small glass of port-wine and a slice of seed-cake, in the manner of everybody's most ancient great-aunts, before he managed to escape from a sermon on the general decay of morals and manners.

His next port of call was very much of a contrast; for he disappeared down a dark and dirty alley, where Miss Carstairs-Carew would have refused to follow him even in thought;

and then into a narrow tenement made noisier by a high and declamatory voice in an attic . . . From this he re-emerged, with a rather dazed expression, pursued on to the pavement by a very excited man with a blue chin and a black frock-coat faded to bottle-green, who was shouting argumentatively:

'He did not disappear! Maltravers never disappeared! He appeared: he appeared dead and I've appeared alive. But where's all the rest of the company? Where's that man, that monster, who deliberately stole my lines, crabbed my best scenes and ruined my career? I was the finest Tubal that ever trod the boards. He acted Shylock – he didn't need to act much for that! And so with the greatest opportunity of my whole career. I could show you press-cuttings on my renderings of Fortinbras –'

'I'm quite sure they were splendid and very well-deserved,' gasped the little priest. 'I understood the company had left the village before Maltravers died. But it's all right. It's quite all right.' And he began to hurry down the street again.

'He was to act Polonius,' continued the unquenchable orator behind him. Father Brown suddenly stopped dead.

'Oh,' he said very slowly, 'he was to act Polonius.'

'That villain Hankin!' shrieked the actor. 'Follow his trail. Follow him to the ends of the earth! Of course he'd left the village; trust him for that. Follow him – find him; and may the curses –'
But the priest was again hurrying away down the street.

Two much more prosaic and perhaps more practical interviews followed this melodramatic scene. First the priest went into the bank, where he was closeted for ten minutes with the manager; and then paid a very proper call on the aged and amiable clergyman. Here again all seemed very much as described, unaltered and seemingly unalterable; a touch or two of devotion from more austere traditions, in the narrow crucifix on the wall, the big Bible on the bookstand and the old gentleman's opening lament over the increasing disregard of Sunday; but all with a flavour of gentility that was not without its little refinements and faded luxuries.

The clergyman also gave his guest a glass of port; but accompanied by an ancient British biscuit instead of seed-cake. The priest had again the weird feeling that everything was almost too perfect, and that he was living a century before his time. Only on one point the amiable old parson refused to melt into any further amiability; he meekly but firmly maintained that his conscience would not allow him to meet a stage player. However, Father Brown put down his glass of port with expressions of appreciation and thanks; and went off to meet his friend the doctor by appointment at the corner of the street; whence they were to go together to the offices of Mr Carver, the solicitor.

'I suppose you've gone the dreary round,' began the doctor, 'and found it a very dull village.'

Father Brown's reply was sharp and almost shrill.

'Don't call your village dull. I assure you it's a very extraordinary village indeed.'

'I've been dealing with the only extraordinary thing that ever happened here, I should think,' observed Dr Mulborough. 'And even that happened to somebody from outside. I may tell you they managed the exhumation quietly last night; and I did the autopsy this morning. In plain words we've been digging up a corpse that's simply stuffed with poison.'

'A corpse stuffed with poison,' repeated Father Brown rather absently. 'Believe me, your village contains something much more extraordinary than that.'

There was abrupt silence, followed by the equally abrupt pulling of the antiquated bell-pull in the porch of the solicitor's house; and they were soon brought into the presence of that legal gentleman, who presented them in turn to a white-haired, yellow-faced gentleman with a scar, who appeared to be the Admiral.

By this time the atmosphere of the village had sunk almost into the subconsciousness of the little priest, but he was conscious that the lawyer was indeed the sort of lawyer to be the adviser of people like Miss Carstairs-Carew. But though he was an archaic old bird, he seemed something more than a fossil. Perhaps it was the uniformity of the background; but the priest had again the curious feeling that he himself was transplanted back into the early nineteenth century, rather than that the solicitor had survived into the early twentieth. His collar and cravat contrived to look almost like a stock as he settled his long chin into them; but they were clean as well as clean-cut; and there was even something about him of a very dry old dandy. In short, he was what is called well preserved, even if partly by being petrified.

The lawyer and the Admiral, and even the doctor, showed some surprise on finding that Father Brown was rather disposed to defend the parson's son against the local lamentations on behalf of the parson.

'I thought our young friend rather attractive, myself,' he said. 'He's a good talker and I should guess a good poet; and Mrs Maltravers, who is serious about that at least, says he's quite a good actor.'

'Indeed,' said the lawyer. 'Potter's Pond, outside Mrs Maltravers, is rather more inclined to ask if he is a good son.'

'He is a good son,' said Father Brown. 'That's the extraordinary thing.'

'Damn it all,' said the Admiral. 'Do you mean he's really fond of his father?'

The priest hesitated. Then he said, 'I'm not quite so sure about that. That's the other extraordinary thing.'

'What the devil do you mean?' demanded the sailor with nautical profanity.

'I mean,' said Father Brown, 'that the son still speaks of his father in a hard unforgiving way; but he seems after all to have done more than his duty by him. I had a talk with the bank manager, and as we were inquiring in confidence into a serious crime, under authority from the police, he told me the facts. The old clergyman has retired from parish work; indeed, this was never actually his parish. Such of the populace, which is pretty pagan, as goes to church at all, goes to Dutton-Abbot, not a mile away. The old man has no private means, but the son is earning good money; and the old man is well looked after. He gave me some port of absolutely first-class vintage; I saw rows of dusty old bottles of it; and I left him sitting down to a little lunch quite *recherché* in an old-fashioned style. It must be done on the young man's money.'

'Quite a model son,' said Carver with a slight sneer.

Father Brown nodded, frowning, as if revolving a riddle of his own; and then said:

'A model son. But rather a mechanical model.'

At this moment a clerk brought in an unstamped letter for the lawyer; a letter which the lawyer tore impatiently across after a single glance. As it fell apart, the priest saw a spidery, crazy crowded sort of handwriting and the signature of 'Phoenix Fitzgerald'; and made a guess which the other curtly confirmed.

'It's that melodramatic actor that's always pestering us,' he said. 'He's got some fixed feud with some dead and gone fellow mummer of his, which can't have anything to do with the case. We all refuse to see him, except the doctor, who did see him; and the doctor says he's mad.'

'Yes,' said Father Brown, pursing his lips thoughtfully. 'I should say he's mad. But of course there can't be any doubt that he's right.'

'Right?' cried Carver sharply. 'Right about what?'

'About this being connected with the old theatrical company,' said Father Brown. 'Do you know the first thing that stumped me about this story? It was that notion that Maltravers was killed by villagers because he insulted their village. It's extraordinary what coroners can get jurymen to believe; and journalists, of course, are quite incredibly credulous. They can't know much about English rustics. I'm an English rustic myself; at least I was grown, with other turnips, in Essex. Can you imagine an English agricultural labourer idealizing and personifying his village, like the citizen of an old Greek city state; drawing the sword for its sacred banner, like a man in the tiny medieval republic of an Italian town? Can you hear a jolly old gaffer saying, "Blood alone can wipe out one spot on the escutcheon of Potter's Pond"? By St George and the Dragon, I only wish they would! But, as a matter of fact, I have a more practical argument for the other notion.'

He paused for a moment, as if collecting his thoughts, and then went on:

'They misunderstood the meaning of those few last words poor Maltravers was heard to say. He wasn't telling the villagers that the village was only a hamlet. He was talking to an actor;

169

they were going to put on a performance in which Fitzgerald was to be Fortinbras, the unknown Hankin to be Polonius, and Maltravers, no doubt, the Prince of Denmark. Perhaps somebody else wanted the part or had views on the part; and Maltravers said angrily, "You'd be a miserable little Hamlet"; that's all.'

Dr Mulborough was staring; he seemed to be digesting the suggestion slowly but without difficulty. At last he said, before the others could speak:

'And what do you suggest that we should do now?'

Father Brown arose rather abruptly; but he spoke civilly enough. 'If these gentlemen will excuse us for a moment, I propose that you and I, doctor, should go round at once to the Horners. I know the parson and his son will both be there just now. And what I want to do, doctor, is this. Nobody in the village knows yet, I think, about your autopsy and its result. I want you simply to tell both the clergyman and his son, while they are there together, the exact fact of the case; that Maltravers died by poison and not by a blow.'

Dr Mulborough had reason to reconsider his incredulity when told that it was an extraordinary village. The scene which ensued, when he actually carried out the priest's programme, was certainly of the sort in which a man, as the saying is, can hardly believe his eyes.

The Rev. Samuel Horner was standing in his black cassock, which threw up the silver of his venerable head; his hand rested at the moment on the lectern at which he often stood to study the Scriptures, now possibly by accident only; but it gave him a greater look of authority. And opposite to him his mutinous son was sitting asprawl in a chair, smoking a cheap cigarette with an exceptionally heavy scowl; a lively picture of youthful impiety.

The old man courteously waved Father Brown to a seat, which he took and sat there silent, staring blandly at the ceiling. But something made Mulborough feel that he could deliver his important news more impressively standing up.

'I feel,' he said, 'that you ought to be informed, as in some sense the spiritual father of this community, that one terrible tragedy in its record has taken on a new significance; possibly even more terrible. You will recall the sad business of the death of Maltravers; who was adjudged to have been killed with the blow of a stick, probably wielded by some rustic enemy.'

The clergyman made a gesture with a wavering hand. 'God forbid,' he said, 'that I should say anything that might seem to palliate murderous violence in any case. But when an actor brings his wickedness into this innocent village, he is challenging the judgement of God.'

'Perhaps,' said the doctor gravely. 'But anyhow it was not so that the judgement fell. I have just been commissioned to conduct a post-mortem on the body; and I can assure you, first, that the blow on the head could not conceivably have caused the death; and, second, that the body was full of poison, which undoubtedly caused death.'

Young Hurrel Horner sent his cigarette flying and was on his feet with the lightness and swiftness of a cat. His leap landed him within a yard or so of the reading-desk.

'Are you certain of this?' he gasped. 'Are you absolutely certain that that blow could not cause death?'

'Absolutely certain,' said the doctor.

'Well,' said Hurrel, 'I almost wish this one could.'

In a flash, before anyone could move a finger, he had struck the parson a stunning crack on the mouth, dashing him backwards like a disjointed black doll against the door.

'What are you doing?' cried Mulborough, shaken from head to foot with the shock and mere sound of the blow. 'Father Brown; what is this madman doing?'

But Father Brown had not stirred; he was still staring serenely at the ceiling.

'I was waiting for him to do that,' said the priest placidly. 'I rather wonder he hasn't done it before.'

'Good God,' cried the doctor. 'I know we thought he was wronged in some ways; but to strike his father; to strike a clergyman and a non-combatant –'

'He has not struck his father; and he has not struck a clergyman,' said Father Brown. 'He has struck a blackmailing blackguard of an actor dressed up as a clergyman, who has lived on him like a leech for years. Now he knows he is free of the blackmail, he lets fly; and I can't say I blame him much. More especially as I have very strong suspicions that the blackmailer is a poisoner as well. I think, Mulborough, you had better ring up the police.'

They passed out of the room uninterrupted by the two others, the one dazed and staggered, the other still blind and snorting and panting with passions of relief and rage. But as they passed, Father Brown once turned his face to the young man; and the young man was one of the very few human beings who have seen that face implacable.

'He was right there,' said Father Brown. 'When an actor brings his wickedness into this innocent village, he challenges the judgement of God.'

'Well,' said Father Brown, as he and the doctor again settled themselves in a railway carriage standing in the station of Potter's Pond. 'As you say, it's a strange story; but I don't think it's any longer a mystery story. Anyhow, the story seems to me to have been roughly this. Maltravers came here, with part of his touring company; some of them went straight to Dutton-Abbot, where they were all presenting some melodrama about the early nineteenth century; he himself happened to be hanging about in his stage dress, the very distinctive dress of a dandy of that time. Another character was an old-fashioned parson, whose dark dress was less distinctive and might pass as being merely old-fashioned. This part was taken by a man who mostly acted old men; had acted Shylock and was afterwards going to act Polonius.

'A third figure in the drama was our dramatic poet, who was also a dramatic performer, and quarrelled with Maltravers about how to present *Hamlet*, but more about personal things, too. I think it likely that he was in love with Mrs Maltravers even then; I don't believe there was anything wrong with them; and I hope it may now be all right with them. But he may very well have resented Maltravers in his conjugal capacity; for Maltravers was a bully and likely to raise rows. In some such row they fought with sticks, and the poet hit Maltravers very hard on the head, and, in the light of the inquest, had every reason to suppose he had killed him.

'A third person was present or privy to the incident, the man acting the old parson; and he proceeded to blackmail the alleged murderer, forcing from him the cost of his upkeep in some luxury as a retired clergyman. It was the obvious masquerade for such a man in such a place, simply to go on wearing his stage clothes as a retired clergyman. But he had his own reason for being a very retired clergyman. For the true story of Maltravers' death was that he rolled into a deep undergrowth of bracken, gradually recovered, tried to walk towards a house, and was eventually overcome, not by the blow, but by the fact that the benevolent clergyman had given him poison an hour before, probably in a glass of port. I was beginning to think so, when I drank a glass of the parson's port. It made me a little nervous. The police are working on that theory now; but whether they will be able to prove that part of the story, I don't know. They will have to find the exact motive; but it's obvious that this bunch of actors was buzzing with quarrels and Maltravers was very much hated.'

'The police may prove something now they have got the suspicion,' said Dr Mulborough. 'What I don't understand is why you ever began to suspect. Why in the world should you suspect that very blameless black-coated gentleman?'

Father Brown smiled faintly. 'I suppose in one sense,' he said, 'it was a matter of special knowledge; almost a professional matter, but in a peculiar sense. You know our controversialists often complain that there is a great deal of ignorance about what our religion is really like. But it is really more curious than that. It is true, and it is not at all unnatural, that England does not know much about the Church of Rome. But England does not know much about the Church of England. Not even as much as I do. You would be astonished at how little the average public grasps about the Anglican controversies; lots of them don't really know what is meant by a High Churchman or a Low Churchman, even on the particular points of practice, let alone the two theories of history and philosophy behind them. You can see this ignorance in any newspaper; in any merely popular novel or play.

'Now the first thing that struck me was that this venerable cleric had got the whole thing incredibly mixed up. No Anglican parson could be so wrong about every Anglican problem. He was supposed to be an old Tory High Churchman; and then he boasted of being a Puritan. A man like that might personally be rather Puritanical; but he would never call it being a Puritan. He professed a horror of the stage; he didn't know that High Churchmen generally don't have that special horror, though Low Churchmen do. He talked like a Puritan about the Sabbath; and then he had a crucifix in his room. He evidently had no notion of what a very pious parson ought to be, except that he ought to be very solemn and venerable and frown upon the pleasures of the world.

'All this time there was a subconscious notion running in my head; something I couldn't fix in my memory; and then it came to me suddenly. This is a Stage Parson. That is exactly the vague venerable old fool who would be the nearest notion a popular playwright or play-actor of the old school had of anything so odd as a religious man.'

'To say nothing of a physician of the old school,' said Mulborough good-humouredly, 'who does not set up to know much about being a religious man.'

'As a matter of fact,' went on Father Brown, 'there was a plainer and more glaring cause for suspicion. It concerned the Dark Lady of the Grange, who was supposed to be the Vampire of the Village. I very early formed the impression that this black blot was rather the bright spot of the village. She was treated as a mystery; but there was really nothing mysterious about her. She had come down here quite recently, quite openly, under her own name, to help the new inquiries to be made about her own husband. He hadn't treated her too well; but she had principles, suggesting that something was due to her married name and to common justice. For the same reason, she went to live in the house outside which her husband had been found dead. The other innocent and straightforward case, besides the Vampire of the Village, was the Scandal of the Village, the parson's profligate son. He also made no disguise of his profession or past connection with the acting world. That's why I didn't suspect him as I did the parson. But you'll already have guessed a real and relevant reason for suspecting the parson.'

'Yes, I think I see,' said the doctor, 'that's why you bring in the name of the actress.'

'Yes, I mean his fanatical fixity about not seeing the actress,' remarked the priest. 'But he didn't really object to seeing her. He objected to her seeing him.'

'Yes, I see that,' assented the other.

'If she had seen the Rev. Samuel Horner, she would instantly have recognized the very unreverend actor Hankin, disguised as a sham parson with a pretty bad character behind the disguise. Well, that is the whole of this simple village idyll, I think. But you will admit I kept my promise; I have shown you something in the village considerably more creepy than a corpse; even a corpse stuffed with poison. The black coat of a parson stuffed with a blackmailer is at least worth noticing and my live man is much deadlier than your dead one.'

'Yes,' said the doctor, settling himself back comfortably in the cushions. 'If it comes to a little cosy company on a railway journey, I should prefer the corpse.'